ARIA DAZE

Rudy Jones's New Year's Resolution

A Happy Holidays Short

First edition

Cover art by David James Blackwell

This book was professionally typeset on Reedsy.
Find out more at reedsy.com

Dedicated to anyone who has spun the block. Time is not an enemy. It is a clever friend.
To my loving husband who I model my book boyfriends after.
(Yes, even the nasty parts.)

Contents

Foreword

This is a novella, which is shorter than a traditional novel. Rudy and Noah's story is still a HEA, but it moves at a faster pace compared to my other work. Please enjoy it for what it is.

Rudy's Plotting Playlist

Cider & Hennessy
The Essential EARTHA KITT
MARIAH CAREY

One

Chapter 1

Noah

"What the fuck!?" I spun around, sending my crossbody knocking into the display of seasonal cookie tins as I did so. Someone had touched me, and not just any kind of touch. I personally feel that the best way to touch someone who isn't expecting it is not at all, but I'd settle for a light shoulder tap if necessary. This, however, was a *caress*. Then, as I instinctively dug around in my bag for pepper spray I noticed it wasn't just someone who touched me. It was Rudy Jones. Rudolph Jeremiah Jones. All six-foot-one of him stood in front of me. His arm was outstretched so his abnormally large hand could shield his cognac eyes from the impending stream of pepper spray. His thick brows and long lashes conveyed his surprise. Then those starter locs with that neatly trimmed beard were the icing on the cake. Still handsome. He always had been, and that thick Bayou accent he hummed with certainly didn't hurt. He was a good Baptist Southern boy, a world-class baker, a grade-A cuddler, and also my ex-husband.

"Lawd, No. You bout to spray my ass down for a lil bump?" he asked.

My goodness, that accent. I had to take a breath to reply. My heart clearly hadn't received the memo that we were divorced. Just the sound of his bass voice had my heart thumping like I was running a marathon. Usually, a brisk walk around Target's various clearance sections had me beat.

"It wasn't no lil bump!" I said, hoping to erase some of my obvious excitement. "You rubbing on my arm like I'm the love interest in a Pretty Ricky video!"

Rudy chuckled while slowly withdrawing his hand. I was happy that I didn't mace him, but I think it would've been better for me if I had. He pinched the corner of his bottom lip between his ivory canine, making me wish for things I had no business wishing for. Things like a proper cuddle, those sinfully delicious snickerdoodles he baked just a little soft, and those contoured lips of his to be pressed against my skin.

"No?"

"Yeah, Rudy?"

"You staring at me real serious. You got a knife in that uglass bag?"

I instantly snapped out of my daze. I was gawking at this man. Deer-in-the-headlights, gawking. He seemed interested, or maybe even flattered, but we were not going back down that path. I came to the cabin to clear my mind and figure out my next move. This was a rebirth. Not a rehashing, and not a rekindling. Re-Birth.

"Whatchu doing down here, Country Boy?" I asked.

Rudy carefully restacked the last of the fallen cookie tins before sighing, "You forgot ain't you?"

I squinted my eyes skeptically. Honestly, I had no idea what the hell this man was talking about. I forgot, but I wasn't going to tell him that. I spent too much time during our marriage fussing at him for forgetting.

"Nope," I answered confidently.

"Hm. Then why you getting firewood?"

I looked down at the firewood I dropped at my feet. I loved a good toasty fire, especially during snowfall. Zinfandel, check. Fancy cheese, check. Firewood, check. Fine-ass-bear of an ex-husband staring me down in the middle of the only general store in a 60-mile radius? Also, check.

"I like to stay warm. The cabin needs some new insulation around the windows."

"Squirrels?"

"Yeah," I groaned.

The cabin was a wedding gift given to us by my late father. He adored Rudy, but didn't necessarily agree with us tying the knot so young. He insisted we weren't ready, but I was stubborn and I did it anyway, so he left us with some advice. "Time away from reality preserves the fairytale." I didn't get what he meant then, but I was geeked to have a fancy Colorado cabin in my possession.

Now at thirty-one, his advice was crystal clear. Love can be a fairytale if you take care of it. But Noah Tyler Senior was right, we weren't ready. Eighteen-year-olds don't know how to take care of much of anything. I certainly wasn't taking care of cars, business, or myself very well at that age. Then marriage was a whole other ball game. You make a promise to a person, stack all your chips on forever, then somewhere between the beginning and the middle you get hit with the reality of the ride. Forever is a long time to go. Especially with unresolved issues.

Being needed was so terribly hard, and I was far too young to be good at it. Rudy was far too young to be self-reliant. So we let unmet expectations fester until they became these rotten sinkholes that were irreparable no matter the amount of dirt thrown at them. I would be selfish, Rudy would shut down, and we'd fight so bad that I would be dizzy from screaming at him. Then we'd have sex, effectively bandaging the problem for then. Only to repeat the cycle months later. Eventually, we didn't have enough to bandage, so we both threw in our ends of the rope and now we were standing face-to-face as strangers with a history. The touch of the man I once adored felt so foreign that I nearly maced him in front of twenty other adults. Life can be so cruel when she wants to.

"You forgot," he chuckled.

"I did," I nodded.

"It's ok. Nala told me you had a lot going on."

My snitching-ass auntie was still telling him my business. She'd been my favorite growing up, but clearly, Rudy had gotten her in the divorce.

"I'm fine. Plans change. I'm in my, *"go with the flow era,"* I shrugged.

Rudy laughed. Audaciously at that.

"Still bad at lying?" he asked.

"Yeah," I groaned.

"Clearly. But you said I could have the cabin for my golden birthday, so I'm here to collect on that."

That's right. Rudy was turning 31 on the 31st of December. He was a New Year's baby. He was always indifferent about his birthday when we were younger, but I promised him we'd have a big celebration in the cabin on his golden birthday no matter what. No matter what.

"Shit! I can try to get an earlier flight back?" I offered. I secretly hoped that my best attempts at beating the chivalry out of him all those years ago had failed. It was New Year's week, and last-minute flights cost a small fortune.

"You ain't got no money for allat, No," he laughed.

Not quite as chivalrous as I hoped. Damn Nala's gossiping ass. I'd deny it if I wasn't so sure of his sources, but that was fruitless considering their standing monthly FaceTime.

"The cabin has three bedrooms," he whispered.

"It does," I nodded.

"We grown folk."

"We are."

"So we'll each take a bedroom, nobody gets the masters, and we'll mind our business. I'll stay out your hair while you do your paper, and I'll also cut your firewood since I know you broke ass can't afford wood and good wine."

I scoffed. I was going to accept because, yes, I loathed cheap wine, but a girl's gotta keep some of her self-respect.

"What's in it for you?" I asked, noticing the delight gleaming in his eyes.

"Nothin', just being nice."

"Out with it!" I demanded.

"Fine," he sighed. "I want you to make me some chicken and dumplings in exchange for the wood."

My sex-starved brain was having a field day every time he mentioned wood. Especially given all those times we did Pinocchio role-play. *He was definitely a real boy.* I jumped at my own perverted delusions before throwing my palm towards him.

"Fine. Chicken and Dumplings, done."

I expected our conversation to be finished but Rudy stepped closer, nibbling that thick lip of his.

"Hey, No?"

"Yes?" I asked.

Rudy chuckled at my dazed expression before pointing out the obvious.

"You ain't letting go of my hand."

I stumbled back in panic, toppling the display of holiday caramel corn and making the clerk groan. Fuck! This was a bad idea waiting to happen. I couldn't spend six days with my ex-husband. I needed to find a hotel.

Rudy

I knew she had forgotten. I knew months ago when I came across her fireplace countdown on Instagram. I could've reminded her then. Part of me wanted to, but a big part of me was excited at the possibility of seeing my wife. Technically and legally, she was no longer mine, but letting go was never my strong suit. That's probably why we're in the situation we're in now. With Noah persevering through shitty WiFi for any hotel close and cheap enough to escape to. She gave her search a good hour, but I think we both knew she wasn't gone spend an hour driving through the snow to spend $280 a night on a hotel without the view, and most importantly, that fireplace.

Noah Sr. had immaculate taste, and he knew his daughter well. Down-filled couches with carved mahogany frames matching the cabin's exterior sat in the living room facing a red brick fireplace. A heavy lift-top coffee table sat between them, and that theme carried through the rest of the house. Down bedding, heavy wood furniture, exposed brick. The cabin was built from the ground up on a plot of land he already owned, and it was still stylish and luxurious thirteen years later. Thirteen years. I met Noah when we were just barely fifteen. My life was hard, but being with Noah wasn't. We'd talk, and laugh, and when she was amiable, we'd dance for hours. Her little body was pressed against my big one and we moved in perfect rhythm. There was no music other than our racing hearts and what we made up in our heads, and I knew I wanted that forever. Unfortunately, forever is a long time. A long time for shit to go wrong.

Noah was no saint, but I accepted that a large part of our divorce was my fault. I had that revelation years ago in therapy. I depended on her for everything and I appreciated nothing. Like most eighteen-year-old idiots, I was looking for a mother, not a wife. But I had met my match with Noah Tyler Harrison. She was raised by a single father with nothing but time, and it was evident. Noah was always assertive. Hell, it's one of the reasons I fell in love with her, but I didn't realize that her assertiveness wouldn't just disappear because I was her husband. So she'd tell me about myself and I'd shut her out. Then she'd get so frustrated that she finally blew up at me over something small. Forgetting about appointments or something. So we fought and screamed, then we'd fuck, and it would all repeat. We got worse because I let us, and then before I could realize it, we were nothing.

Now I was watching the woman who should have been elated to spend some alone time with me accept defeat knowing she had to.

Cruel.

"Maybe I should've reminded her." I thought. But then Noah stood with a yawn to discard her coat and get comfortable. She had on a real pretty gray sweater dress that had a little keyhole for her newly acquired bosom. Her body had changed so much since we got divorced. She was always a bit heavier on the top, but she had evened out and now everything was heavy.

Especially that ass. Noah's ass had always been a marvel, but the new weight gain had me seeing double. So I was a little glad I ain't remind her. Real glad actually.

"I'm gonna go cut ya wood," I announced.

I had to find something to do other than stare at her. Especially after I noticed how big her eyes got every time I said wood. Damn, Pinocchio role-play.

"Ok, I'm starting dinner," she mumbled.

One thing about Noah, she was good on her word. She was willing to make me chicken and dumplings even though she had a long flight from La Guardia and then an hour cab ride immediately after. She was probably exhausted like I knew she would be.

"I already cooked. You can work on your desertion."

"Dissertation," she corrected.

"Same thang," I shrugged.

I watched her nervously peer into the kitchen, blowing those zig-zaggy curls out of her eyes as she did.

"Whatchu cook?" she asked cynically.

I made the one thing an honest Southern Belle couldn't resist.

"Gumbo with all the fixins," I beamed.

I guided her into the kitchen with my hand on her back. She was softer than I remembered. So soft. I bet her ass was even softer. Man, what I would've given to go lower. I popped the lid on my crockpot before fetching a clean spoon and then I got her a good bite ready. Sausage, rice, shrimp, and onion altogether, then her mouth widened to eat the whole spoonful. I watched her glossy lips cling to the spoon and I was sweating afterward, no fire necessary.

"Wow. Um, wow. When did you start cooking?" she asked.

She went back in for more before I could answer, confirming that I had done a good job.

"After me and you split. Ain't wanna burden no one else," I whispered.

I said that and she dropped the spoon in the damn pot. You would've thought I was proclaiming to be the second coming of Christ the way she was staring at me. She made no effort to hide the fact either, she was just gawking.

"You ain't a burden," she whispered.

Her voice was assertive, but reassuring and kind. Still, she was wrong.

"Not no more, but I was. It ain't right for a grown adult not to know they can't wash reds and whites together. Sorry about your Zeta Phi dress by the way."

I ain't know what to expect with the way she was looking at me. Maybe she'd accept my apology. Maybe she'd tell me about myself. I'd be fine with it either way. Age has given me the gift of new kinks. Bossy women happened to be one of those.

"You still owe me," she grumbled. "Go cut my wood."

The fire was burning strong and the embers were crackling loudly. Almost loud enough to cover Noah's absentminded snoring. She had been dozing off for an hour. I'm assuming it was my handiwork since she ate three bowls of gumbo, and a nigga was proud. Even if she was fighting her sleep. Noah's head dipped onto that chest of hers while her maple syrup eyes rolled shut. She'd breathe normally for a few minutes, then she'd start snoring, wake herself up, type a few more words, and do it all over again. Some things never changed. Noah never believed in rest, she believed in perfection. That had always been clear. The woman was working on her second Ph.D. after all. Nala tried flattering me, telling me it was cause Noah missed me, but I wasn't buying it. She was in pursuit of excellence, hoping to prove to everyone that she deserved the life she had. Hoping to prove that she was capable. Hoping to prove that she was worthy. Maybe even hoping that she'd start feeling those things herself.

But I couldn't take it after her third nod. Her body and her brain were fighting a war her brain wouldn't win. I waited until her fingers stopped twitching to collect her. I almost wanted to hide that damn laptop for the weekend, but I was willing to settle for eight hours instead. First on the agenda though was getting rid of them uglass glasses that snapped back in the middle. She had regular glasses, but she preferred those when she was "in the zone." Why she was insistent on running around looking like somebody's grandmama, I'm not sure, but I couldn't stand them things.

I took off her shoes after removing her geek gear, and that was nearly the death of me. See, I really liked feet. Especially my wife's. They were small and she had perfectly squared toenails that descended in an even slant. FootBook be damned. No one was beating Noah Tyler Harrison-Jones. After spending too much time looking at her ruby-red toes, I picked her up and put her over my shoulder. I expected her to fuss at me, but she ain't move a muscle. I think she had finally crashed.

"I'm real glad you couldn't find a hotel," I admitted.

Clearly, she needed this just as much as I did. I walked through the house quietly, trying not to wake her. All was going well, but then she reached out to hold my hand when I tucked her into bed. I could tell it was her subconscious impulse taking over, but I was powerless to stop it. Her touch was still euphoric for me after six years, putting me into a natural high. After the year I had, I needed that. So maybe we still needed each other.

Two

Chapter Two

Noah

I have a problem. Most teenage girls' celebrity crushes were always normal. Usher, Maxwell, Zac Efron, maybe even Corbin Bleu. Do you know who my celebrity crush was and still is? Craig Robinson. So damn fine. See, I really got a thing for bears and I always have. So when everybody was telling me that I shouldn't date Rudy because he was too big, I was essentially deaf. I liked what I liked. Evidently, that was consistent. Rudy had changed a bit with newly defined muscles and a stronger jaw, but he was still firmly in the Plush Pals category. Then it didn't help that I knew he was big everywhere. **Everywhere.**

"Please don't masturbate to a sex dream about your ex-husband," I told myself. "That ain't right."

I ain't even know I was asleep until I woke up hot and bothered after a rather lucid dream about Rudy fucking my throat. I guess there are consequences to celibacy. Consequences such as the visceral ache in my pelvis that was screaming at me to go jump Rudolph Jones's bones. I knew it'd be worth it too, that man's dick was immaculate. Especially when he…

"Stop it!" I chided, fighting my wild thoughts.

I stared at the ceiling in delusion before the swing of Rudy's ax brought me back to reality. He was already outside chopping wood for the day. I really wanted to shower and change clothes, especially since my dress was fighting for its life because I had been living in it for twenty-four hours straight, but what did I do instead? I got up and walked my nosey ass right to the window, eager to enjoy the show.

Rudy's back tightened while his strong arms sprang up, and then his shoulders took over the rest of the work when he swung down, splitting a log into thirds. It was a captivating motion, and I watched him for far too long. His rich skin contrasted sharply against the bright snowy hillside. His brow beaded with sweat as his arms swung. His lips were tucked into themselves, aiding his concentration. It was simply picturesque. Then the chill of the frosted glass brought me back to reality. My entire face was pressed against the window in search of the best possible view. Just like that, my mind was illustrating those strong arms swinging me around. I stopped staring and scolded myself. That could not happen. I didn't go backward. Only forward.

"This ain't a rekindling," I told myself, finally padding to the bathroom.

Hellishly hot water splashed against my tight muscles sending a warm mist to revitalize my dry curls, and I groaned. It was exactly what I needed. I enjoyed the warmth enveloping my body before I started to lather up. I pumped too much soap on my rag, but I needed to strip my skin. Especially after last night. I couldn't believe I fell asleep in airport clothes. Filthy-ass airport clothes. I watched an older man sneeze in his hand before pulling a shop door open. Absolutely disgusting. *Wait.* How did I get into bed? I don't remember taking off my shoes, or glasses, or tucking myself in. The last thing I remember was butchering the word syllogisms four times while my eyes fought for the right to close. "Son of a bitch. He tucked me in," I said to myself.

Rudy's presence was definitely a surprise, and his lax and inviting demeanor was astonishing. Especially given the way we left things at our final hearing. Especially given what I said. I was angry. I was truly and wholly angry. I had lost my best friend, my lover, and my life partner all at once, and I had gone out kicking and screaming. *"Maybe if you'd been raised right, we wouldn't be in this situation!"* I hissed. It was cruel, especially then. Rudy's upbringing was no more his fault than it was the sky's fault for being blue. But I was overwhelmed, and I needed to place the blame on something. Anything to get me through the painful reality that had become my life. Empty bed, empty fridge, empty heart.

So when he popped back up yesterday, all smiles after what I considered to be a shit show grand finale, I was more than shocked. He seemed excited, almost happy that I had forgotten. Not at all perturbed by the possibility of us being in each other's space. I was mostly stressed. It had been six years and I still wasn't over him. I still missed the way he smelled after spending all day outside. Like clean sweat, pine, cinnamon, and that damn cherry wood cologne. I still shivered when I heard his voice early in the morning and late into the evening. When it was raspy and coated with sleep. I still missed the way he touched me. He was the first to ever do so, and those moments were still vivid in my mind, replaying at my every inconvenience.

Do you really ever get over your first? Apparently not, because I was busy servicing myself to those same ethereal visions of Rudy touching me. Gentle, confident, and slightly disrespectful at times. I was a puppet in his palms, especially when he talked his shit. Some women liked to be called a good girl. I preferred to be called Duchess. Not sure why, it just scratched an itch in my bratty brain. NOLA men had the praise game on lock, especially with that accent. Deep and smooth, and speech wholly improper. Just like my thoughts. I strummed my clit a little faster while I imagined those full upturned lips kissing that spot between my neck and collar, him marking me as he did countless times before, and me bending at his whim. Then I finally came. Then I was out of breath and doubly unsatisfied. Damn, Rudolph Jones.

After slathering my parched skin in a pound of lotion and oil, I left the safety of the bathroom to find a comb for my hair. It needed to be doing something other than whatever this was because I wasn't gonna detangle the shit twice. I was successful in my search, but my feet wouldn't carry me back to the haven of the locked bathroom. They couldn't. We were immobilized by something akin to enchantment. Rudy had brought in the wood and his merlot skin was glistening with well-earned sweat. He stacked the logs neatly before lifting the corner of his rust thermal Henley to dry the sweat off his brows, essentially giving me a free show. He was thick in all the right places with a soft tummy, wide, muscular chest, and hips that could brace the sudden category-five hurricane my clean panties had become. "Jesus," I mumbled, too shameless to stop myself.

Rudy finally looked up, jumping as he did. Maybe my presence was unexpected, maybe it was my expression. Whatever it was, he was thrown for a loop.

"No, you good?" he asked.

I stood to collect my breath before clutching my racing heart.

"Yep, just ready to be done with this paper."

He locked eyes with me and his lips curled into a smile. An audacious, knowing smile at that.

"Oh, okay. Your laptop is in the coffee table. I'mma take a shower."

"O… okay," I mumbled, trying to restrain a creeping visualization of a sudsy Rudy.

"I'm gone write."

Rudy gave me a thumbs up before stalking to the bathroom and shutting the door, allowing my feet to once again move my body. I threw my hair in a platts and a scarf, donned my grandma glasses, and opened my laptop. Then I stared at the dim screen in absolute pwnage. Damn, Rudolph Jones.

Rudy

I think my wife has a crush on me. I never thought I would ever say that, but the way she just looked at me made me feel ass-naked. She looked at me like this plenty of times before, but this felt like the first time. New and anxious, and unawarely reciprocal. Like she wanted something she might not be entitled to. When really, all she had to do was ask. She could ask and I would be putty in her lil hands. She could ask and I'd right every wrong I've ever done. She could ask and I would give her everything I hadn't the first time.

We had grown up. Six years' time will do that to you. Especially six years living without someone you needed. I had needed her then too, but that was different. It was wrong. I knew it, she knew it, Jesus knew it. I wanted her domestic and hidden away, sometimes out of jealousy, sometimes out of ignorance. My folks hadn't taught me much else. Women belonged at home while men worked. It was a very cut-and-dry gender expectation. But Noah wasn't raised that way, and her expectations were much different. Noah wanted a partner, equal in every right. She needed me too, but not in the way I was comfortable with. So when we reached the point where neither one of us was willing to bend, I forced her hand.

"I took a job," I told her proudly. Noah's concentration instantly severed and she glanced up from her sprawling assessments with concern, not pride.

"What? What happened to school?" she asked. *"You didn't think to run this by me?"*

I hadn't, because I naively thought I was head of our household. All authoritative, all-knowing.

"No, Noah. I'm your husband, you ain't mine!"

Her curls whisked away from her eyes violently while she loured at me.

"Excuse me?"

"I'm in charge. I wanted to take a job, so I took a job. We ain't gotta live like…"

"Stop talking," she hissed. *"You think that I would rather be alone in a big-ass house, maintaining it by myself, than be in an apartment with you by my side? Rudolph Jones, I know you ain't that damn slow!"*

I had no counter to her actual argument. She would've been alone. I would've been over the road for three months at a time, and she couldn't come with me because she was still in school. I had known that, but I accepted the contract anyway.

"Undo whatever it is you just did," she demanded.

Sure, I could've called HR and told them I actually couldn't leave my wife alone for three months after her father just died, but that ain't what my pea-brain self did.

"I can't undo it, Noah. Contracts already signed, the bonus hit my account this morning."

She laughed, but it was really more of a scoff. It was cold, frustrated, and so ear-splitting that it still haunts my nightmares. Then she stood and backed away from the cramped dining room table.

"Then you might as well sign these divorce papers to celebrate your shiny new salary. I'm done."

I had destroyed a seven-year marriage in an instant, and I knew it as soon as the words left my mouth. Noah had been by my side through everything, and I was too pigheaded to do the same for her. I wanted to provide, because that's the only way I knew how to be a husband, and she needed a partner. Someone to cry to when the days became too much, someone to run her a bath when she was drained, someone to meet her where she was. I was so concerned about being a failure as a man because my wife made more money than me, that I failed as her friend. Which was far more important to me than anything else. So I had spent the last six years watching Noah blossom behind a screen. At first, I spent six years trying to force myself to forget about her. Eventually, I spent six years learning, unlearning, grieving, and appreciating. Then, fed up with the idea of going through the motions with someone else, I became too bold and met my wife where she was. Like I should have years ago.

So here we were. With my wife, who is technically, and legally not mine, typing away on some long-ass paper while I plotted against her. I wondered if she still liked Snickerdoodles. My recipe had gotten better. A lot better since then. I was busy scrubbing sap from under my nails when I heard her shrill scream, and I abandoned all of my plans immediately.

"Duchess! You aight, girl?" I called, wrapping myself in a towel.

I ran into the living room to find Noah banging her head on the table, laptop covered in sticky brown coffee.

I caught her forehead in my palm before she could hurt herself further. Some things truly never change. Even if you prayed they did. Her face was red and irritated. Her brow bone was swollen from the senseless beating, and her eyes were wet from a defeated sob.

"It's ruined! I ruined everything," she cried.

She was understandably upset. She had been working on that Thesaurus for months, but I still couldn't let her hurt herself. So I pulled her away from the table, into the rocking recliner.

"You ain't ruin nothing," I said, pulling her onto my chest.

"You don't know that," she sniffled.

"You save yo work?"

"It autosaves. But my laptop is still fried. I can't afford a new one."

"You ain't ruin nothing," I repeated. "I'll fix it for you. We'll see if we can find some parts."

I hated school when we were younger. I hated the schedules, I hated the material, I hated the people. Teachers, students, and lunch ladies alike. Couldn't stand them. Too many questions and rumors. Too much truth in some of them. So when we graduated, I had sworn off repeating the process with college. I went to trade school for my CDL, and that was after serious pushing from Noah. However, I needed something stable to occupy my time after the split. So I enrolled in a tech-repair apprenticeship and that eventually kickstarted my career as a computer hardware technician.

"What are you talking about, Rude?" she sighed.

"I learned a few things these last few years. Namely how to replace motherboards and keyboards. So we'll put yo laptop back together, good as new, then you can finish that long-ass encyclopedia you been writing."

She laughed. It was so good to hear her laugh. It was infectious and consuming, encasing me like the warmth of a summer sun. So I joined her in jest before she nuzzled her little pointed nose in the crook of my neck. I jumped, and Father God above, I wish I hadn't. Because it made reality hit her like a train. She gasped and then sprang from my lap like I had the bubonic plague.

"Sorry," she muttered.

I sat quietly, saying nothing. I wasn't sorry, not even in the slightest. I even started to protest before I noticed her eyes dart down to my lap.

"Rudy Jones, put on clothes. You up here exposing yourself to every livin' creature in a ten-mile radius!"

I looked down to find my towel had slipped when she sprang out of my lap. I still wasn't sorry. I was glad actually. Real glad.

Noah

Rudy found a similar laptop model for sale within two hours, and he had negotiated them down to a fair asking price since it was for parts anyway. He was going to handle the transaction, but he made me get dressed and go with him. Saying something about me needing space away from the scene of the crime. So I got dressed and followed him out to the truck. I was happy to go if that meant stopping in the apothecary on the way back. Plus I think he was right. My tense shoulders relaxed while I took in the beautiful snow-covered mountainside, almost forgetting about the fast-approaching deadline and coffee-filled laptop. Almost. The deadline was still looming, but it became manageable while Rudy absentmindedly rubbed my knee.

Eventually, I was dopey from all the serotonin his touch was providing. Dopey to the point of blissful ignorance. I had no idea where we were, how far away we were from town, or how long we'd been driving. My focus was being dually divided between the picturesque mountain range and Rudy's euphoric touch. That big hand of his completely encased my kneecap while his thumb rubbed just below it. His palm was soft besides a few calluses. Some old, some new, all distinguishable to me, all welcomed. But I panicked while feeling something more familiar than I wanted it to be. His absence. Rudy took his hand off me to throw the truck in park, and I was left in the passenger's seat with my body demanding he return his hand to where it rightfully belonged. Funny how some things never change.

I was glad Rudy insisted on handling the exchange. Online marketplace meetups always made me uneasy, but this dude was a stage-five creep. His black-rimmed eyes shifted over to the truck a few times, accidentally catching my gaze. Then on the third and final time, he licked his cracked lips, drawing Rudy's attention. Rude said something belligerent, making the creep retreat into his little damp dwelling, and then he stormed back to the car, laptop in hand. Those thick lips were curled into a menacing scowl the entire time.

"Everything alright?" I asked nervously.

Rudy didn't immediately answer. He put the car in drive first, then exhaled his frustration.

"Muhfuckas is so damn weird. I hope I don't ever get a daughter cause I'm definitely going to jail."

I started to sing Let's Go To Prison with laughter, and although visibly apprehensive, Rudy did eventually laugh.

"You a very unserious woman for all them fancy degrees," he chuckled.

"And is. Don't nobody wanna be a stick in the mud all the time. It's exhausting," I confessed.

I expected him to say something smart, but he returned to quiet, letting the hum of the engine narrate our drive. He did, however, rub my knee again, and that was all the reassurance I needed.

Rudy left me to my own devices at the apothecary. One of the many things I loved about Heaven's Peak, Colorado was the local artisans. There was a coffee roastery on Main Street that sold every flavored bean you could possibly think of, my favorite being peach bourbon. Then there was the local tailor, whose wife was also a seamstress. Gorgeous fabrics were draped into equally exquisite gowns, making me wish I wasn't always so busy. If I ever got the funds, I was buying that damn red satin dress. The corsetry was amazing. Tailors, cobblers, and grocers alike, I was obsessed with the stores here. I could spend hours shopping here and I had done so before, but then there was the apothecary.

Smythe's Fine Apothecary lived up to the name. A heavy red carved wood door hung at the entrance to my personal nirvana, and I had fallen in love the first time I stepped inside. To your immediate left was a wall of a hundred bath bombs. Some were seasonal and rotated with the holidays and trends, some were staples, and quite a few were my personal favorites. They were all carefully and thoughtfully labeled, and displayed in gleaming glass jars with turn knobs. Reminiscent of old-school jawbreaker machines. To the right, there was an equally impressive wall of soak salts and scrubs. All color-coded, bright, and beckoning. They also had refill stations for their most popular bubble baths and shower gels. With various incense, lotions, oils, and body tools, all calling my name.

Unfortunately, I was broke. I was in school, and I had gotten fired from my day job as an analyst a month ago after sleeping through an alarm. This wasn't a regular occurrence for me, but I was so tired that I slept fifteen hours straight. Then I didn't call them back because of anxiety, and I got hit with a no-call no-show. I cried, begged, and pleaded, but the firm's answer remained unchanged. My father had left me some money that I could survive on if need be, but it was by no means extravagant. I needed a job, and I was without one. So on the sixth anniversary of my divorce, I celebrated by being unemployed and feeling dually discarded. It had been a rough year.

So although I was dead ass broke with less than $400 in my account, I shrugged and bought two bath bombs. My favorite, which is named after the owner's wife, Glory, then something classic, a French vanilla latte. I looked around for a while longer before spotting Rudy at the door. He was scrolling on his phone, holding his own bag of goodies. He rarely indulged in expensive bath products, so I wondered who they were for. Wait, did he have a girlfriend?

I ain't even think to ask when I agreed to spend a week with him, although I'm sure he hadn't just dried up in my absence. I tried to shake the feeling off, but my anxious brain took a stroll down memory lane, reminding me of all the ways he used to apologize. In the garden, in the car, once in the library. Had he been doing that to someone else? I scowled, glancing at the full bag tucked into his curled hand. I really hoped those were for him.

"Ready?" he asked.

"Unfortunately," I sighed.

Rudy flashed me a gentle knowing smile before getting the door and guiding me out.

"I know what'll cheer you up."

We were parked in front of GelHouse, the local nail salon, fifteen minutes later.

"You want a pedicure and a fill-in? I'm paying," he whispered.

I looked down at my lifting acrylic in shock. This felt intentional. This whole day did. I didn't have to remind him about the wood, he had brewed me coffee, and he had gotten me outside of my head. First by dangling a trip to the apothecary in front of me, now with the nail salon.

"What are you up to?" I asked.

A smirk teased his lips, threatening to undress me where I sat if I kept staring.

"Nothin'. I want one too. Come on, we can catch up."

He unbuckled my seatbelt and slid out to grab my door, smothering the chance for me to probe further. Like I said. Intentional.

Rudolph Jones has a thing for feet. He has for a while, maybe even his whole life. I found out when we were sixteen. I was getting ready to be deflowered in the bed of his pickup when he put my big toe in his mouth, and I was appalled. Most girls my age had thought head was the freakiest you could get, and there I was with my toes in a boy's mouth. Then why did it feel so good? It felt way better than I thought it would. My nerves were on fire while he swirled his warm tongue against the tender pad of my toe, and I almost didn't notice him easing into me. *Almost.*

Remember what I said about Rudy being big everywhere? Yeah, that was true even back then. I immediately winced when he tore through my hymen, dancing on a very thin line between pleasure and pain. I guess my body was overwhelmed though, and a tear slid down my cheek, abruptly pausing all motion. *"Shit, Noah. I'm so sorry,"* he gasped. I shook my head trying to gather enough breath to talk. He had knocked the wind out of me, but it wasn't unpleasant. *"Please don't stop,"* I murmured. Rudy tucked his wonderfully thick lips into his mouth before slowly easing out of me. So I had to put my feet up on his chest to redirect his attention before he was successful, forcing him to finish what he started. *"I'm a big girl,"* I chuckled. *"I can take it."*

Why was I thinking about our first time in the middle of a crowded nail salon? Rudy was staring at my feet while we soaked for pedicures. I ain't notice at first because the massage chair was working its magic on my tight back, but I was tickled when I did. I thought the Baptist in him would have some shame, but clearly, I was mistaken. He was looking at my feet the same way he did the very first time he looked at them. Lustfully. If we weren't in public, I might have even put them in his mouth again. Wait, that sounded an awful lot like a woman thinking about fucking her ex-husband. Thank God for the distraction of others. I was suddenly grateful for the people buzzing around us. Rekindling be damned!

Rudy

Green is my favorite color. Always has been. I remember asking my parents to paint my room green when I was five, blissfully unaware that paint cost money. But I had made up for the white walls at thirty-one. My house was green, my truck was green, and my wife's little toes were now green too. Emerald green at that. The kind of green that made me want to do some very undignified thangs in the bathroom of that establishment. Maybe she caught on and this was her way of torturing me. Maybe it was her innocent subconscious. Either way, I needed to say a prayer for my thinning patience when I laid down tonight.

"What have you been up to?" I asked, attempting to redirect my attention away from her feet. She rolled her eyes at my question before sighing. We both knew I knew. Nala kept me up to date on all things Noah, even when she probably shouldn't have. I get it though. Noah was closed off, and I was a reach away if anything went terribly wrong. I was the only good family she had left in the country. Noah Sr. was gone, Nick was a dickhead, and Nala was living her best life in Germany.

"Let's not sit up here and pretend like my auntie ain't been telling you all my business," she chided.

"She don't tell me all yo business," I laughed.

"Hmph," she grumbled.

"I'm serious! She ain't tell me about that time you got a yeast infection cause yo old roommate used your dildo."

I accidentally said that a little too loud and Noah's high-yellow face turned bright red with rushing embarrassment. I knew I ain't have no business saying that in the first place, but I did anyway. Revenge for the toes.

"Rudolph Jeremiah Jones!" she whisper-yelled. "What has gotten into you?"

She checked around the other stations to see if anyone had the privilege of hearing that before scowling at me. She had been doing that a lot lately. Which was weird because it was going well, all things considered. I laughed at her angrily scrunched brow before rubbing her knee.

"Sorry, Duchess. Just fucking with you," I laughed.

I expected her to fall quiet in anger, but she sat up straight and surprised me.

"You got a girlfriend?" she blurted out.

Her question made me pause. Why was she asking? Was she interested? Could she be jealous? I hoped she was jealous. She was always a lil rough when she was jealous. I bit the center of my bottom lip just slightly before smirking.

"No, Duchess. I ain't got no lady friends. You got a man, Cher?"

I knew she didn't, but I had to fuck with her. Besides, that was always the thing that did her in. Being called Cher. She believed it was being called Duchess, which might have been true, but Cher made her squirm in her seat and flex those pretty ass toes. Damn it. I was back to looking at her feet.

"Please put yo shoes back on," I grumbled, fighting off the demon perched on my shoulder. That nigga was telling me fuck the plan, and I almost listened.

Noah put her shoes back on and I joined her in the waiting area for a chair to open up. She was fidgeting again. Maybe she was nervous. Maybe she was stressed. Possibly hungry. I checked the time, noting that it was definitely lunching hours.

"I'll be right back," I said, much to her apparent displeasure.

Her eyes sparkled when I returned, but it didn't seem like it was for the food I had. It felt like they were sparkling for me. I borrowed a chair to sit next to her while her Christmas acrylic was filed down. "Hungry?" I asked.

"Starving actually," she nodded.

I smiled and pulled a box of loaded cheese fries out. Then I got a fork to feed her a few bites.

"Thank you," she mumbled between chews.

Cheese sauce stained her nose from her impatient nibbles, smearing while she spoke.

"Not a problem, Cher," I chuckled.

She got full halfway through the order, and I finished the rest alongside my burger. She had been telling me about her encyclopedia the entire time. She was almost done with her physics doctorate, and man did she earn it. She spoke so fluently about atomic mass, string theory, and inverse quantum generation. Despite only understanding a third of what she was saying at any given time, I was still very interested. Her conviction and excitement was palpable, and that made me happy. It was like we were the black gender-bent, Leonard and Penny.

Her nails were finished forty minutes later, and despite the devil I knocked off my shoulder earlier, I really wanted to see those mocha brown and gold stilettos wrapped around my dick. I had to leave a good tip for that. Ten out of ten for bringing forth the wild thoughts that would consume me for the next three years. But something else was on my mind while we headed for the truck.

"Why'd you ask if I was seeing somebody?" I asked, opening the door for her.

I knew the answer I wanted, and I also knew I was very unlikely to get it. Noah has never been that forthcoming.

"I was jealous," she shrugged, climbing into the truck.

I stand corrected. Noah was never that forthcoming *before.*

"What do you mean you was jealous?" I asked.

Noah ignored me, instead choosing to turn on some music while the truck warmed. But my brain was itching to find out if I had a chance. Even if it was a lil one.

"No, what could you possibly be jealous of?" I asked, holding her thigh.

Noah wiggled underneath my grip before her eyes slid up to mine. Her gaze was so sharp it cut my heart into two, inclining me to give her the bigger half.

"You keep touching me," she mumbled.

I was touching her a lot, but it wasn't necessarily on purpose. I honestly couldn't help it. I spent a long time not touching her, so I think my subconscious was making up for the lost years. Still, I withdrew my hand and apologized,

"I'm real sorry, No. But what's that got to do with anything?"

Noah kissed her teeth irritably. Like she was debating on whether or not I was really that stupid.

"I don't like to share. You not finna be touching me then going home to touch somebody else."

She don't like to share? I'm not finna be touching her then someone else?

Was this my opening? Because if so, I was about to take it the way my mama took my money out my birthday cards. In other words, quickly.

"Whatchu scared of sharing?" I asked.

Clearly fed up with our brief game of chicken, Noah pressed her head to the window and stated her commands.

"Take me to the store. I need to grab a few things for dinner," she whispered.

I listened, hoping it would get me points in the event of her answering my earlier question. Besides, I needed stuff too.

Chapter Three

I fixed Noah's laptop in just under an hour when we got back. It powered right back up like the coffee spill never happened. I was excited to show her, but she was in a groove. She always got into a groove when she was excited to cook. The kitchen was humming with savory sizzles, boiling pots, and classic R&B. If she had answered my earlier question, I'm sure I would've been in there with her, holding her waist and swaying to Maxwell while she cut her dumplings. Now Noah Tyler Harrison-Jones was the worst baker I'd ever met. Her cookies tasted like erasers. Her brownies were crumbly like mulch. But for some reason, her dumplings were heavenly. They were soft and pillowy, and they cradled that onion-rich gravy just right. She also cut them the perfect size in my opinion, because if you had a proper spoon you could scoop up an entire dumpling, a shred of chicken, and a chunk of veggie all in one bite. I had missed my wife, of course, but living without those dumplings was also torture.

"Come taste this, Rude!" she called.

I got my big ass up at lightning speed as soon as she said my name.

"Right here, Cher!" I exclaimed, rubbing my palms together like Birdman.

Her lips pursed to blow on a spoonful, enchanting me where I stood, then she extended her magic to my mouth, urging me to try it. I did and it was wonderful. I think I melted into the floor because it was that damn good. Rich, salty, umami perfection. Her dumplings were just as tender as I remembered, practically dissolving after just a few chews. Then that gravy? I could drink that shit by the carton.

"Rudy, you ok?" she asked, shaking my arm.

I came back to reality, noticing her concerned expression.

"I'm good, real good," I whispered. "Are you ok, Duchess? I asked in bliss.

Noah relaxed her shoulders slowly, taking my wrist in her small hand. Then her thumb lazily traced my tendon, as if the motion was calming her own racing heart.

"You scared the shit out of me. It looked like you was having a stroke for a second there."

I had to laugh, because as callous as she pretended to be, it was painfully evident that she still cared. It was painfully evident that we both did.

"I'm good Cher, I promise. Just excited and grateful that you cooked for me is all." I took the liberty of pecking her forehead before making plates.

"Thank you," I whispered.

Noah

Rudy fixed my laptop, and it was better than when it was new. It was ridiculously responsive, the keys weren't sticking, and my screen was actually staying bright. I giggled in delight while he cleared the bowls from the table. Dinner was good, both the food and the company. Conversation flowed between us effortlessly, just like it did when we were kids. My day had gone well, and now all I needed was something sweet. Maybe Rudy would make cookies if I asked. I saw him pick up a few things when we were in Piggly Wiggly. Lord knows I can't make cookie dough to save my life. I was working on my formatting when Rudy came in with a rag and a can of Pledge. Then he went to work wiping down the tables. *"What the hell?"* I thought. I remember having to fuss at him plenty of times for leaving behind a mess, and now he was just absentmindedly wiping sparse crumbs from the table. I stared at him in disbelief, wondering what the last six years had done to my husband.

I worked for an hour, hunched over the table like a scholarly goblin while furiously typing away. My fingers pressed against the keyboard with new urgency, but my word count was still unremarkable.

Typical.

I probably needed a break, but healthy coping habits ain't really my thing. So I continued working until the sweet scent of warm cinnamon flooded my nose. Rudy had baked. I started to call into the kitchen after him, but he emerged carrying a well-stacked tray. Four small mugs rested in front of a plate of still-warm cookies while he sat across from me.

"I thought we'd try a hot chocolate flight," he said.

I glanced at the drink tags he carefully labeled. Caramel Irish Cream, Chocolate Covered Strawberry, Mint Chip, and Moonshine Mocha. They were ripped straight off an Instagram post I shared months ago. Like I said earlier, intentional.

An hour later I was buzzed. Nope, I was drunk. Two boozy hot chocolates and a glass of sangria later, I was drunk off my ass, and with the fireplace crackling behind me, I was getting hot. I wanted to peel off my clothes, but Rudy reclaimed my attention by offering me the last cookie. I rushed to accept, and although I knew it was improper, I talked with my mouth full, "These are so damn good. I think your recipe got better."

Rudy nodded while his thick lips pulled into a captivating grin.

"It did. I changed some ratios and bake times," he confessed.

"Ah. Cookie math. You always have been real smart."

It was true. Rudy was incredibly intelligent. He was just lazy, which drove me nuts. But I remember when I was falling apart at twenty, and for a brief moment it felt like we might make it. He read my assigned readings out loud so I wouldn't fall behind, he double-checked my work, and he made sure I was eating enough so I wouldn't perish. He was a good husband, he was just fickle. As soon as I got back to normal, so did he, and it made me wonder if

I had erred by rushing to be ok. Rudy was capable, just unapplied. He was consistent that way back then.

"You give me too much credit," he said, yawning.

His cognac eyes pinched shut from exhaustion, and his voice heavied with sleep, dampening my panties further.

"Imma put everything away and lay down," he said, collecting the mugs.

I stared at him while he did so before something urged me to grab him. So I did, wrapping my hand around his thick wrist while we stared at each other. We gazed at each other longingly, like we were both free falling into something we probably shouldn't. I leaned closer hoping he would brace my tumble, hoping his lips might ease some of my need. But Rudy was a gentleman, and he stopped me with a gentle peck on the temple.

"Night, Noah. Get some rest," he whispered.

He departed quietly, leaving me at the table with heat rising through my center. It should've been what I wanted but it wasn't. I wanted my soft pressed against someone's hard. I wanted to smell cold pressed hemp oil on locs. I wanted full upturned lips to be pressed onto mine. I wanted Rudolph Jones.

I don't remember taking off my nightgown, but I did. The pink and yellow flannel gown piled at my feet before I made my way out of my room. It was a good decision according to inebriated me, and so was this. I stood in Rudy's doorway briefly before stalking over to the left side of the bed. He wasn't snoring yet, but I knew he would be soon. So I slid under the heavy comforter quietly, but my cold feet grazed Rudy's, making him jump.

"Whatchu doing, Duchess?" he grumbled drowsily.

"You," I said, brimming with liquid confidence.

Rudy sighed before putting a pillow between our bodies. Then he ever so gently brushed the curls out of my eyes. "No, ma'am. You drunk. I wasn't raised right, but I wasn't raised all the way wrong."

His reply hit me in the chest like an arrow. Partially because he wouldn't have sex with me, mostly because he remembered me saying that shit to him.

"I should have never said that to you," I whispered.

Rudy sighed, then rubbed my shoulder, easing some of the tension from rejection.

"You was hurting. I understand. You was also kinda right."

I shook my head. No matter how I felt, I shouldn't have lashed out like that. What happened in his childhood wasn't his fault. No one chooses their parents. Hell, I ain't choose not to have a mom.

"Duchess, I hurt you. We used to be best friends, and I essentially pissed on our relationship with kerosene because I was a young dumb boy. A person can only take so much heartbreak. So while it hurt when you said that, it was also my fault. We even, trust me," he mumbled.

I pressed my chin against his waiting palm, then I stared into those easily intoxicating earthen eyes.

"We are not even. And that wasn't right of me. It's not your fault that your folks were who they were. And I knew that, so I shouldn't have thrown it in your face."

Rudy chewed his lip momentarily before pulling back, obviously sharing my frustration.

"Now I kinda wanna fuck you," he chuckled.

I wiggled closer and got excited feeling his half chub resting against my thigh.

"Will you?" I asked, ever hopeful.

"Night, Duchess," Rudy laughed.

Ugh. I was hungover. My head was pounding, I was dehydrated, and while my body should have been sore, it wasn't. Maybe because Rudy was holding me. He was keeping me together while I fell apart. God, it felt good to be held. He was warm and heavy, and those big hands of his were resting on my waist and hips. Then the way his dick pressed against the curve of my ass? One word; magnificent. I wiggled against his frame, eager to fit my entire ass into his lap. Wait, what was I doing? I was wrapped in my ex-husband's arms after drunkenly trying to fuck him, that's what. After I swore to high heaven I wouldn't. Plus I hadn't even made it forty-eight hours. I was hopeless.

I needed to leave this man's bed before he came to collect the check I wrote him last night. Mostly because I would cash it. I would cash it in an instant. My mouth was dry, but my pussy wasn't, and goodness did Agnes miss Rudy. Especially the way he smelled. Pine, cherry wood, and warm cinnamon. I pressed my nose to his forearm and took a little sniff. I swear his smell was an elixir meant to transport me to my personal heaven. A heaven filled with snickerdoodles, bath bombs, and Rudy Jones's slight overbite smile. Which is precisely why I needed to leave. I wiggled out of half of his hold, freeing myself from his waist grip, but my hips were a different story. I tried to roll out of bed and he locked me in place, pulling me back to his core. The same thing happened when I tried to move his arm. Ugh. Damn me and my love of bearish men. I had fallen right into a bear trap.

I swallowed my pride and reached for his hip to wake him. Rudy had always been real ticklish in the hips. My fingertips lightly grazed his warm exposed skin and he jumped awake, freeing me from his clutches.

"Leaving so soon, Duchess?" he yawned.

Damn that deep sleep voice. He almost made me want to climb back under the covers with him. *"Nope, focus on your paper!"* my monologue hollered.

"I'm hungover, and I need to eat something so I can finish my paper."

Rudy sat up, towering over my medium frame and demanding me to meet his gaze.

"You sure that's all you wanna finish?" he asked.

His hand grazed my cheek while he tucked a curl back into the bonnet he insisted I wear last night, and like a fool, I whimpered.

"I think I can help you boost your productivity," he said, leaning forward.

I wanted him. I wanted him so bad like fire wanted air. But that was the problem. I always did, and there was no guarantee this time would be different. I couldn't go through that again. Six years without talking to someone I adored? No, thank you. I sprang from the bed immediately, but I was shocked to find I was completely naked, titties swinging, and coochie undeniably sticky, giving a show to the man I was trying to deny. Damn drunk Noah for taking off that nightgown. Rudy's eyes flitted downward just long enough to be noticeable before he climbed out of bed to bring me his robe.

"Go start your day, Duchess. I'll leave you alone," he laughed, pecking the top of my head.

I scrubbed a layer of skin off in an effort to dampen my longing. My ex-husband had held me, tried to kiss me, then stared directly at my crotch which had opened like a morning glory for him. God. Maybe I should've masturbated. I had a good dildo in my room, but if Rudy heard me I think I would die. Maybe he'd bring me back to life though. If he could snatch my soul out, what was stopping him from snatching it back in? *"No! Absolutely not!"* I told myself. I cannot fuck my ex-husband. I cannot fuck my ex-husband. I cannot…I really, really wanted to fuck my ex-husband.

Rudy

It was so fucking cold and I ain't even grab gloves. Honestly, it was probably better for me. I needed some cold air to keep me from going crazy. Noah was so warm. Her body, her gaze, clearly her box. Her shit was open like a spring flower, inviting me to stick my nose in her for a sniff. Man, what I wouldn't give for a sniff. Even just a lil one. Am I disgusting? Yes, absolutely, but really only when it comes to my wife. I've been in other relationships since we split, but it was never the same. They all got some weird, overly polite, half-baked version of me, and don't even get me started on the sex. It was lukewarm like formula, even when I tried, but most of the time I didn't. See, sometimes I wanted sex from those women, but I needed it from Noah. I needed to touch her. I needed to make her whimper, cuss, and cry. I needed to be so deep inside her that I ran the risk of drowning in her desire. I needed her wrapped around me so that I could stay tethered to this world. I needed my wife.

I decided to split all the firewood we would need for the rest of the week so I could concentrate on getting my woman back. I hoped it wouldn't take too long because I was starting to lose my shit. I ain't never been one to take advantage of a drunk woman, but I caught myself telling Noah to put it in my face last night. Then this morning? I thought her toes were bad, but I could've passed out seeing her thighs. Noah was always a baddie, and age only aided that. Them hips and dips and curves was gone get us in trouble. Possibly even remarried if I played my cards right. Probably pregnant if her shit was still as sticky as I remembered.

I grabbed a big log next, and even though I'm a big boy, that muhfucka had me lifting with my knees, not with my back. It was fine though, it was only a couple of feet to the chopping stump. Unfortunately, I looked up. I looked up and right at the living room window where Noah stood naked, moisturizing those mile-long legs. She was still in my robe, and she had kept her scarf tied over her edges. I was always a sucker for scarves and bonnets. Especially if they was pink. Her waist twisted slightly when she moisturized her toes and I damn near came where I stood. She was the definition of perfection. Even Uncle Luke's girls ain't have shit on Noah.

I guess she felt me staring and she caught my gaze. I expected her to cover up, or scowl at me, but she gave me a little wink instead, and that did me in. My knees buckled first, then I lost my grip. Which caused me and the log to fall backward into the frozen snow. It hit me square in the chest, knocking all the wind out of my lungs.

Shit.

My life was aight, I guess. If Noah was gonna be the thing to end me, I was willing to bump it up to good, maybe even great. Still woulda wanted a sniff. Oh well, people in hell want ice water.

Just when I was willing to accept my time, I heard Noah stomping across the frozen yard with urgency. Shit, maybe I did have a chance.

"Rudy!" she screamed.

I threw an arm in the air to let her know I wasn't dead, but I was stuck there. I wiggled underneath the log before a 5'7" fury of a woman pushed the damn thing off my chest and onto the hill.

"Rudolph Jones! You scared the shit outta me!" she hollered.

I probably shouldn't have been smiling considering I almost died, but I did. She ain't even put on clothes to come rescue me. She was still nearly naked in my bigger-than-average robe and a pair of snow boots. Eyes wide, hair everywhere, titties swanging.

"I'm ok, Cher," I said, reaching for her cheek. "Besides, if I woulda died, you woulda been set for life."

She looked at me like I was in my final moments before snatching my big ass off the ground.

"We going to the hospital," she hissed, leaving no room for protest.

I laughed and followed her audacious tail back to the cabin for the keys. God, it hurt to walk. Mostly because my chest was on fire, but partially because my menace of a wife's hips were swaying under that robe. Back and forth like the motion of a bow on a violin. There was a new log weighing me down. The one that was actively pressing against the zipper of my Levi's.

Noah didn't like driving. I'm guessing that's why she moved to New York after we split. It's "walkable" or whatever she be saying. It's also high as hell and the farthest she could get from me since I was still in Houston, but I let her keep her reason. She also didn't like hospitals. I knew that was because Senior spent the last year of his life in them before his unfortunate passing. Heaven rest that man's soul. So Noah avoided those two things like the plague. Driving and hospitals, and also bad news. Then I went and dropped a log on my chest and she was forced to face two out of three, with the final likely not far behind.

"It's just a bruised rib," the doctor announced, motioning to my X-ray. "You definitely have some inflammation, but it should be manageable with some ibuprofen and rest," she explained further. Rest? Fuck. I was right, bad news. That meant no chopping or driving, or likely fucking. Even though I'm sure my chances of fucking were slim to none now.

"Can he have sex?" Noah asked.

Now I know the sound I made was ugly because I felt it, and it hurt, but Noah ain't acknowledge my obvious shock. She just kept staring the doctor down, waiting for an answer.

"Misses…?"

"Doctor, Harrison-Jones. Yes."

Not her setting the record straight! God, I'm a blessed man. A dumb one, but blessed nonetheless.

"Yes, sexual activity is fine as long as it doesn't irritate the rib or become too strenuous. So no lifting or bending."

That ugly sound left my mouth again. Because no this woman didn't sit up here and assume I be lifting my wife. I mean I do, but that ain't the point. What a very unprofessional, yet accurate, assumption.

"Sounds good to me," Noah replied.

I bet it did to her freaky-tail self. Not that I'm complaining.

"Alright. We'll wrap this up, get some discharge papers, and get you all out," Doctor I-know-you-fold-your-wife-like-sheets said.

I sat quietly in my assless gown while Noah asked about her remaining concerns, drawing up a few questions of my own.

"Why you ask that lady about sex?" I blurted out.

Noah started the truck before rolling her head toward me, cutting her eyes as she did.

"Why you say I was gone be set for life if you kicked the bucket?" she replied.

God, I hated when she answered a question with a question. Then she knew I did because she smiled at me. Bratty ass.

"You answer my question first then I'll answer yours, woman."

Noah shrugged dismissively.

"I asked cause I wanna fuck you. Your turn."

My chest hurt again, but I don't think it was my rib. I think it was my heart kicking into overdrive. I just sat still, mouth open like a catfish before she nudged my shoulder.

"Your turn," she barked.

No she wasn't rushing me after dropping a bomb like that. I wasn't thinking about what I said hours ago, I was thinking about getting my dick wet right now. In the backseat of this truck while defying the doctor's every order. But her brows scrunched so right I could see that vein in her forehead. Man, she was fine when she was pissed off.

"You the beneficiary on all of my insurance policies," I shrugged. "If I get sent to the upper room, you become a thousandaire. Actually, you get the house too, so you a hood rich millionaire, Cher."

She stared at me for a long time. A real long time. Maybe too long. It started scaring me after a while cause she wasn't blinking.

"Why would you do that?" she finally asked.

"I wasn't leaving it to Charlene and Henry," I laughed.

"My ashes would be put in a Payless shoe box. Plus I ain't leaving them folks no house. I ain't that damn healed."

"Rudolph Jones, we ain't married no more," she grumbled.

Yes, I knew that. I spent the last six years regretting it. But together or otherwise, I made a promise to Noah to always take care of her, and I was sticking to it. Even if it took me a little while to figure out that caring is more than just providing a check.

"I know that, Cher. But I'm always gone look out for you. That ain't never gone change."

Noah shook her head before going quiet to rake through her thoughts. Her eyes moved back and forth over the dash like she was arguing with herself. Like I knew she probably was. I ain't know exactly what she was thinking about, but it felt like it was heavy. I was almost concerned until she laughed and whipped out of the parking spot.

"You got condoms?" she asked.

"Yes," I whispered, slightly embarrassed. "I'm not a whore. I just knew you'd likely spend the week with me."

Her eyes went wide before she stuck out that pouty bottom lip, pulling all my focus to her mouth. Duchess always had a pretty mouth. Perfectly kissable lips, and a slightly crooked right canine that I wanted to lick.

"Rudolph Jones, you been plotting on me?" she asked.

I ain't have no more pride left so I gave up the act.

"Yes, Duchess. From the minute you posted that fireplace countdown," I admitted.

Chapter Four

Noah

Rudolph Jeremiah Jones is a menace. Always has been, and probably always will be. I remember when we were sophomores in high school. We shared biology and college algebra together, and sometimes we saw each other at lunch. I was real quiet and bad at making friends. Then I was a girl named Noah. No one was interested in a girl named Noah. Rudy was big, and funny, and troublesome. He was also smart, but so damn troublesome. He'd joan on anybody for any reason. Even the teachers. Especially the students. And while that shoulda made me nervous, it didn't. I felt safe around him. Comfortable even. So on the days when our lunch periods overlapped, I'd go over to him and listen to him joan on everybody. Eventually, he stopped noticing other people though, and he spent most of his lunch talking to me. Laughing, joking, whispering.

Eventually, I got bold, and when I had a real long day, I'd just sit on the bench behind him and lay my head on his back. He'd hum to me sometimes, ask about my day, ask how my daddy was doing. This went on for weeks until I couldn't find him at lunch one day. I was excited to tell him about my project. I'd won a National Junior Physics award, and for some reason, he was the first person I wanted to tell. So being deprived of that soured my mood, and I went down the hall sulking before freakishly big hands pulled me into an empty classroom. Rudy was standing there with a single daisy resting in his hand. It looked like he had picked it recently, and he handed it to me with a nervous grin before tucking my frizzy curls out of my eyes. *"I like you,"* he said. *"I like you real bad, and I think you like me. So since we like each other, we should go together."* As a devout wallflower, I had no idea what to say, so I did the one thing my brain was hollering at me to do. I leaned in and I kissed Rudolph Jones on the lips. Then he kissed me back. Then we were stuck with each other.

Nothing much had changed sixteen years later. We were still stuck with each other, even after failing miserably at being apart. Rudy quietly sipped lobster bisque while I worked on my pot pie. I wanted to hurry up and finish eating. The food was good, but it wasn't really what I wanted in my mouth. Yes, I know I said I wouldn't fuck my ex-husband, but the man still had me in his will. He deserved a lil pussy for that. Plus it didn't help that I could see his print through that paper-thin hospital gown. I had been ready to go ever since the doctor clarified the nature of his injury. Shit, I had been ready to go since his dick was pressed on my back this morning. I probably would have got what I wanted too, if I hadn't jumped the gun and flashed him. Damn, my impatience.

I hadn't learned my lesson though. The waitress came by with the check and I rushed to pull my wallet out. Forgetting two important things. One, I was broke. Then two, Rudy was southern, and not just in proximity, but also in mannerisms. He smacked that card out my hand so fast my head spun.

"Absolutely not, Duchess," he hissed. "It's bad enough you have to drive."

He finally noticed the waitress was staring between us like she just witnessed a crime, so he clenched his jaw and whispered discreetly.

"PutyomfmoneyawaybeforeIfalloutinhere."

He hissed it out all at once and it was effective in putting me back in my place. Rudy side-eyed me the entire time while pulling a few bills from his wallet. Then once that nosey-ass waitress left, he started his bullshit.

"You been paying niggas for dick, Duchess?" he asked.

"Rudy Jones!" I chided.

"No Ma'am! You ain't finna Rudy Jones me up in here."

"It's not that serious! It was twenty-five dollars," I insisted.

"It is that serious!" he scoffed. "Senior woulda cocked a double barrel down outta heaven and shot me where I stood!"

"Ain't no guns in heaven," I laughed.

"A lighting bolt then. Shit, a hard-ass rock. Something! Don't you ever do that again," he fussed.

I tried to withhold a smile and failed. Then I sighed while gazing into my husband's eyes. He was so very serious, and also mildly concerned that this was a regular habit of mine. Those cognac eyes rippled with laughter and care. It was sweet. It was endearing. It was also making me wet.

"You right, I'm sorry. You want me to make it up to you with some pussy?"

Rudy's expression muted and I thought he might be about to pass out again, but then the entire booth moved a few inches while he stood to collect me.

"You make it real hard for me not to be an exhibitionist," he mumbled, pulling me from my seat.

I was learning patience at the big age of thirty. I guess Rudolph Jones was full of surprises. I thought we'd go home, get naked, and jump right into the action, but that ain't what happened. Rudy brewed us some tea, then ran us a bath, and now I was sitting in between his legs, shoulder-deep in a Hibiscus Harlot-infused soak. The apothecary stuff was for me. My gut was right. That day was very intentional. I honestly thought the intention would stop or at least pause once I agreed to fuck him, but it hadn't. Soft 90s R&B played over the speakers while Rudy squeezed fragrant chamomile hair oil into his palm. Then those heavy fingers of his parted my thick curls to rub my scalp. Intentional? Yes. Effective? Very. Let's hope my birth control could keep up with his effectiveness.

He whispered affirmations to me while he tenderly massaged my crown.

"You are so kind. You are so smart. You are so breathtaking, and you are also inappropriate," he laughed.

Did I know those things to be true? Yes. Did hearing it out of Rudy's mouth make me want to dissolve into the water? Also yes. Words of affirmation are just as valid as the other love languages. Especially for me. Especially now. I rubbed the pads of my fingers over Rudy's strong upper thigh. His rich skin was still visible underneath the deep burgundy water and he still smelled like himself. Pine, bourbon, and warm cinnamon. He smelled like peace. A peace I never wanted to leave again.

"Can I tell you something?" I asked, leaning back onto his chest.

"Anything, Duchess," he nodded.

I scratched through that thick winter beard of his for a little while before continuing. It was wonderful to touch him again, and I wasn't in a rush to relive the past. Then again, I didn't want to repeat it either.

"I thought it'd be like this the first time," I admitted.

Rudy took a deep breath, one that made him wince. One that made me nervous.

"Me too, Cher," he whispered. "But I think we was too young. We needed to figure ourselves out first, then each other."

Funny, that was the same thing Senior said. He was right. I never got to tell him to his face, but he was absolutely right. We could have saved years of strain and heartbreak by just listening. I guess that's youth for you. You be thinking you grown. Thinking you know everything.

"I'm sorry," I mumbled.

Rudy kissed my temples just as tenderly as he did this morning. Just as intentionally.

"Ain't no thang, Duchess. I'm sorry too," he whispered.

Should sex make you nervous? Even if it's with a person you fucked before?

To be fair, I ain't fucked Rudy in some years. I ain't fucked nobody else in a while either, and they certainly weren't worth being nervous for. I had put up with my fair share of terrible partners. Bad strokes, no rhythm, dry kisses. One nigga had the audacity to tell me he ain't give head! We are too big and grown for that. Then there was Rudolph Jones. A man so nasty that he made me blush from memory. Toe-sucking, navel-licking, ass-eating, fuck-me-into-the-mattress, Rudy Jones. How I ain't end up somebody's mama by now is beyond me. Then again, I'm happy I'm not. He stressful enough.

"How ya rib feeling? I asked. We were just sitting in towels and talking, but I was getting impatient. Especially since I could see under his towel.

Rudy did a lil wiggle in order to give me an accurate report.

"Not bad. I think the ibuprofen done kicked in."

Thank God, because I was ready. I sat in his lap and kissed him so eagerly I wasn't sure where I was after a while. I was just confused, excited, and desperately wet. Like a Labrador that got lost in a rainstorm.

"Slow down, Duchess," Rudy chuckled, nibbling my bottom lip.

"I really don't wanna," I moaned.

And I didn't. I wanted to make up for lost time. I wanted a reminder of why I ain't drop this man's last name in the six years we were apart. I wanted my husband inside of me, and I was tired of slowing down.

Rudy chuckled while trailing my collar. Those lips of his were crafted by God himself. Thick, pillowy, and oh-so distracting. Because he had flipped me over onto my back before I could realize it.

"Rudolph Jones! The doctor said no strenuous activity!"

"That was hardly strenuous," he laughed.

I squinted at that smug grin of his. I guess we were in the business of lying.

"I'm two hundred pounds!" I hollered. "That's a load!"

Rudy just chuckled while making his way down to my breasts.

"Ok? I'm two eighty-five, and I'm about to put a load in ya."

I wanted to scold him, but I couldn't. Mostly because his mouth was full with my nipple. God, his tongue felt so good rolling over me. I truly couldn't recall why I ever wanted to deprive myself of the feeling. Oh yeah, I think it was pride. Welp, that was short-lived.

Rudy wrapped his big hand around the base of my titty, massaging it gently while his tongue darted over my hardened nipple. His eyes were focused on me and the very ugly whimper that was coming out of my mouth, and he was smiling the whole time. He was unholy for a church boy. Especially how he made me speak in tongues. Especially how I was calling out for The Father, The Spirit, and The Holy Ghost. What was that thing about blasphemy again? I can't remember, but if God ain't want his name used in vain, he wouldn't have created men like Rudy Jones.

"Fuck, Rudy!" I cried. He was playing me like an old-school Bop It! One of his hands was working my tit that wasn't being sucked. The other was playing with my box. Slowly stretching me open one finger at a time and telling me to come hither. I was trying my best to hold out on cumming, but then his thumb circled my clit and he forced me to.

"Rudy, shit. Please, please, please, please."

I was begging and pleading while he overwhelmed me. But he was still sucking my titties, still rubbing my clit, and still pumping me with those abnormally big fingers. I came again.

This time it was so hard I saw stars. Shit, stars, solar systems, and galaxies. God, why did I ever waste time with pride? Then Rudy made it seem so easy like he had a Noah Tyler Junior instruction manual or something. Shit, the way I kept nutting on his hand, maybe he did.

"Look how sticky you is, Duchess, baby," he said, lifting his digits to my sightline.

I caught my breath while watching my wetness drip from his fingers. Then I choked watching him use it to jack himself off. That dick of his was something. Perfect, in my humble opinion. Thick, upward curved, paved with veins down to the head, and long enough for it to touch my belly button when he slapped it on my waiting pussy.

"I missed you, Duchess," he said, nibbling my bottom lip.

"And so did my friend," he whispered, motioning to his dick.

His heavy, hot, throbbing, and aggressively hard dick. Rudy Jones's shit was menacing to look at, and I'm pretty sure my flight or fight reflex should have kicked in cause it was definitely about to do some damage. Thank goodness for mild ASD though, because the urge to stop him was out the window.

But he was just teasing me, slowly dragging that heavy ass dick between my folds, making me twitch with anticipation.

"Rudy, we done did enough beating around the bush," I whined.

He raised one eyebrow and smirked at my unintentional pun. My pussy had a TWA since I ain't have the plans or money for a wax, and I was frustrated, but I could admit it was funny. We shared a snicker before Rudy leaned forward and whispered against my kiss-swollen lips. His expression changed from amusement to urgency, and so did his tone.

"See, Cher, here's the thing," he whispered while tracing my navel. "I've been patient for a real long time. Then you been posting pictures in them dresses, titties all out, teasing me with these cute-ass green toes," he said, massaging my feet.

"So I think I'mma take my time, and you gone lay back and enjoy it."

Who was I to fight off a hungry bear? I could barely open a salsa jar most days. I bought an Amazon gadget for it, actually. So was I going to push Rudy Jones off of me while he was in the middle of ravaging my coochie? Nope. But not because he said so. I just couldn't pry him off me. Especially not when he sucked my pearl like it was a bomb pop fresh off the ice cream man truck in the middle of an August heatwave. Messing with folks' food can get you killed, you know? Never mind the fact that he was making me cum so hard that I was actively blacking out. Or the fact that seeing my stickiness drip from his beard while he smiled at me was being permanently committed to memory. Completely irrelevant.

Twenty minutes later my heart was beating so fast I thought I might explode.

Then he left my pussy to suck my toes. Three at a time while his thumb rubbed my clit. Then I found out that my early concern wasn't misplaced, because explode I did. My back arched off the mattress while thick warm liquid poured out of me and oozed down my ass. I'm sure I screamed, but I wasn't able to hear it. My body blocked out all of my other senses to keep me from imploding, so I couldn't hear, taste, or smell, all I could do was focus on Rudy's touch. He once claimed to be an unserious student, but that was clearly a lie. Cause he was now a master of me, and he was teaching the class.

Rudy stopped long enough to laugh at me while I lay out nearly vegetative.

"I forgot you can squirt and cream at the same time, Duchess," he cooed, stroking my sensitive folds.

"Rudy," I panted breathlessly, seeking amnesty.

"Don't Rudy me, Cheré. You said you wanted to fuck me. Did you forget what hunching me was like?"

I laid completely still. Hoping that he'd see me all pitiful and exhausted and stop toying with me. Then I watched his thick lips tick upwards into an unserious grin.

"I think you did, but don't worry, Duchess," he whispered.

He rolled a condom on before leaning down for what I thought was a kiss, but I realized it wasn't when he pushed our pelvises flush. He stretched me out like a cheap dress, and God, it hurt in the best way possible.

I gripped the sheets to try to tether myself back to the land of the living while he made his dick jump inside of me, and then Rudy made it worse when his warm breath tickled my exposed throat.

"I'mma help you remember, and I'mma make sure you never forget," he chuckled.

"What?" I moaned. I think he was talking to me, but that thing happened again. Rudy Jones had overstimulated me so badly that my other senses were shot. It had happened a few times in the last hour or so. All of my mental and physical ability was being funneled into touch. Just touch. Like the way his lips touched mine. All slow and purposefully, with his tongue seeking mine during breathless kisses. Then there was the way he touched my waist. His arm was wrapped around me so tight that I was aware of my own breathing. I think I could even feel the ridges of his individual fingerprints against my skin. But I didn't mind him holding me so tight because it kept me from falling apart. Because the way he was touching my insides was consuming.

Thwack. Thwack. Thwack. If we had neighbors, they'd likely think he was beating my ass. All you could hear was skin-on-skin while he pounded into me. He was fucking me on his tiptoes, and his strokes were so deep and rhythmic that they drowned out the buzzing from the vibrator he held to my clit.

"I said I think yo spicy microphone is better suited for duets than solos," he laughed.

Two days ago I thought I was being discreet about my midday masturbation. Turns out I was wrong. I was painfully wrong because Rudy walked his ass right into my room, pulled my underwear drawer open, and grabbed my wand. He had been torturing me with it in every position since and now I was in his lap with my back pressed against his chest. This was the third change after he wore my goofy ass out in missionary and prone and I didn't even remember switching positions. Hell, I ain't even know whose room we were in. I could hardly remember my full name. I did forget what fucking him was like, but I think that's because my brain could not remember with how overwhelming he was.

"How you still going?" I cried.

I remember talking to my sorors who were still on the market after I tied the knot. Most of them complained about the endless supply of minute men while I had the opposite problem. Rudy Jones could keep going forever if you let him. Why? I'm not sure. All I know is that he's some type of rare magical unicorn that can nut and keep fucking. He says it's because my pussy is so good that he doesn't want to stop, but I think he was made specifically to torture me. I must've done something pretty fucked up in a previous existence. Why else would my shy ass be permanently tied to a man this nasty? Sometimes he'd whisper reminders into my ear in public and I'd damn near cum. I'd be all red, hot, and bothered while somebody granny was staring at me in the produce section. Some would call it a blessing, but having to carry extra underwear in your purse for basic grocery store trips is definitely a curse.

Rudy stopped kissing my neck to suck my ear instead, making me scream silently while I suffered through another countless orgasm.

"You want me to stop, Duchess, baby?" he snarled.

Did I want him to stop giving me the best dick of my existence? Not really, but I was hungry as hell. Probably dehydrated too from the way the sheets were looking.

"Yes, nigga. You about to kill me!" I shouted, sitting forward.

"Don't be dramatic, Duchess. You ain't gone die from no seventeen lil ass orgasms."

SEVENTEEN!? The nigga was counting? Most people would be content with two, and here my selfish ass was bussing seventeen times. Damn, Rudolph Jones!

"What is wrong with you?" I spat.

Rudy nuzzled my neck while closing the space I tried to create between us. My back was now firmly against his front while I fell in and out of consciousness. Sex had never been this consuming before. I was cumming so hard that my eyes crossed, my words slurred, and my heart skipped. Then I must've been transported to Deluluville cause I had the audacity to believe he'd take pity on me, but the only relief he gave me was a satisfied smile.

"I missed you, Noah. I missed holding you, kissing you, being inside you while you squirt all over my big-ass country dick. Don't you miss cumming all over your dick, pretty baby? Making a mess?" he asked.

To answer his question, yes. Yes, I did. I could barely make myself cum twice and another man doing this to me was out of the question. Was my husband also a menace? Yes. Yes, he was. He'd been fucking me for hours, had busted thrice, and he still wasn't satisfied. He said something else but I once again lost my senses to an orgasm. Eventually, I came back to reality though.

"Rudy, stop this. You have quite literally fucked the daylight out of me! It's dark outside!"

He looked out the window in sudden realization.

"Oh, yeah. We should probably get dinner soon," he shrugged.

How we were gonna do that in our current position was beyond me. His nasty ass would probably try to drive with me on his dick if he could though.

"I guess I gotta eat something other than pussy to take my meds. So how about you do me a favor, Duchess?" he asked.

"Anything," I answered.

Rudy laughed before repositioning us and pushing me towards his feet.

"How about you ride my shit so I can watch my dick slide in and out of this creamy pink pussy?"

Like I said, filthy. If God was truly watching, I'm sure this would make him look away.

"Yo pretty ass make me nut in five minutes or less, I'll leave you alone."

Fuck, this was not the time for an ultimatum. I was about to die.

"Rude," I gasped.

"Aw, you can do it, Duchess. I know you can do it, baby. Bounce that fat ass for me, Cheré. Lemme see you squirt on it and I'll be good and leave you alone."

Rudy used some of my natural lube to put his thumb in my asshole and I bounced. I bounced hard, high, and fast while singing his name. Eventually, the feeling consumed me, leaving me addicted to the sensation of Rudy Jones. The glide of his skin, the rough grip of his hands, and the sound of that deep, smooth, improper voice. Then, with one minute to spare, I earned myself dinner.

Rudy

Noah was putting shit away. She had eaten two sides of macaroni, fried corn, a bowl of greens, and half my ribs. I was impressed. Impressed or turned on. Probably both. My shit was definitely hard when she slurped down the last of her tea, but then she caught me staring.

"Stop looking at me like that," she ordered.

"I'm not looking at you like nothin'," I laughed. "This how I always look at you."

She must've realized that meant I was always in the mood to do something to her because she turned red-hot before refocusing on her dinner. God, my baby was so pretty sitting up here. She was swaying with the music, shaking hot sauce on her greens, smiling at me. I don't think I'll ever see anything prettier than her smile. Unless she gives me some kids or something. That was a later thing though. I was happy to be where we were right then.

I paid for dinner after threatening to fake a heart attack in the middle of them people's restaurant. My Duchess had her pride, but she was shy, and I was gone use that to my advantage if I needed to. We was walking back to the truck when she stopped me and pulled me close. The town was still done up for Christmas with elaborate ornaments, tinsel, and glittering lights hanging off every building and fixture. It was magical, and it's one of my favorite things about Heaven's Peak. (Besides Noah.)

There was a street lamp above us, and she pointed out how someone had tied mistletoe around it. I really did think my wife had a crush on me. Because wet snow was caking in her fresh twist out, I had squandered a whole day of dictionary writing for her, and she still wanted to kiss me. I pressed my mouth to her soft heart-shaped one and melted. I, Rudolph Jeremiah Jones was on top of the world. I was perched on top of that muhfucka like a crow on a line, and I don't think anything could've fucked it up.

Except it did.

She kissed me again, making my heartbeat in my ears, and I couldn't help myself.

"I love you," I whispered.

"Shit!" I wasn't supposed to say that.

I couldn't even fully process my fuck up before Noah pulled away, pushing off my chest with enough force to hurt my rib and break my heart.

"Wait, Noah," I said, pulling her back toward me.

Noah's lip was tucked into her mouth for safekeeping when she faced me. I expected to see irritation or maybe even disappointment, but those big brown eyes were full of panic. I knew that look anywhere. She was scared. She was scared of me, or what I said, or maybe both. Maybe she was scared of us. Maybe I had fucked it up.

"Let's… let's get home so we can get some rest," she stammered.

She walked back to the truck, leaving me and my racing thoughts under the now dim street light.

Fuck, I ruined the plan by flying too close to the sun.

Chapter Five

Rudy

I have always been what folks call, "sensitive." I remember this kitten I had when I was seven. She was just about as black as me. She had big yellow eyes, pink toe beans, and a weird purr that sounded like a busted bike. So I named her Harley, and Harley was my girl. I even took some work digging out weeds in our older neighbor, Ms. Lucille's garden so I could get her food and litter. I'd have a bad day at school after getting lit up for wearing the same pants two days in a row, but I'd come home and Harley would curl right up on my lap, purring her lil heart out.

Then someone was being evil and killed her. Threw a brick at my baby. I found her up the street after she didn't come home two days in a row, and I cried my heart out while digging her grave. I visited her every day for a week straight. Just came out and sat with her, talked to her. But on the eighth day, Charlene came outside shortly after me and yanked me off the ground by my collar.

"You ain't finna keep crying over no damn mangey-ass cat!" she hollered, popping me.

"You a boy, and I ain't raising no soft-ass cry babies. Take yo ass in the house!" she ordered.

I did as she said, and at the tender age of seven, I learned that no one gave a damn how I was feeling. Especially if it was an inconvenience.

So imagine my surprise when Noah, who had been avoiding me since I accidentally said I love you the night previous, slid into bed behind me. She didn't say anything at first, she just stroked my nape. Her fingertips grazed a few short curls while she moved in a windshield-wiper motion. Then she moved to my shoulders, rubbing firm circles as she descended my spine. I can't lie, the shit felt good, but not good enough to make me forget about last night.

"What you need, No?" I asked.

Noah sucked in a breath so sharp it sounded like a wince, then she sighed. She sighed forcefully enough to warm the tip of my ear with her minty breath. Then she spoke.

"I'm sorry, Rudy."

I scoffed. Her apology did not make me feel better, nor was it what I wanted. *"What do you want then?"* I asked myself.

Truthfully, I knew the answer. I just wanted Noah to know. Actually, I *expected* her to know, and therein lies the problem with our dynamic. My expectations.

"You don't have to be sorry, Duchess," I whispered, attempting to contain my tears.

One fell anyway, and Noah wiped it on cue as if she knew it would fall. How she knew that and not the other thing was beyond me.

"Rudy," she started. "It's not tha…"

I froze, partly hoping she would just put me out of my misery. There was too much hope lingering in her cliffhanger. Too much for me to cling to.

Then she shouted.

She screamed, shouted, and pounded her small fist against the mattress, undoubtedly frustrated.

"This is complicated! We are complicated! You can't just pop back up after six years and suddenly tell me you love me!"

It wasn't sudden. I never stopped loving her, and I ain't regret it. Not even a little bit.

"Well, first off, it wasn't really sudden. You fed me, then fucked me, then fed me again. What'd you expect? Ain't you say men was simple creatures, Cher?" I asked.

Noah screamed again.

"Rudolph Jones! You are not funny!"

I was. I was real funny. Kept me from hurting as bad.

Kept me from crying and being sensitive while my wife seriously underestimated the depth of my love for her. But then she kissed me. She kissed me so hard and fast that I think I got a concussion. Mostly because my thoughts was way too incoherent for it to be anything else. All I could really think about was how good her lips felt on mine, how supple her skin was, and how soft she was in my arms. I always wanted her to be this soft with me. I always wanted her. I wanted her with me. That's what I wanted. A side effect of being sensitive I guess.

Noah finally pulled away after "accidentally" grazing my eager third leg through my pajama pants. Then she sucked her teeth in irritation. I could tell her mind was running a mile a minute. That little nose of hers was scrunched into a thoughtful grimace before she pinched the bridge of it.

Then she screamed again.

"Wash ya ass and put on clothes, Rudy! No sweatpants," she chided.

I'm sure she said that because we were going into town, but I had to fuck with her.

"So you don't want me but I can't advertise? Cold, Cher," I joked.

That vein in her forehead throbbed before she launched a water bottle at me. Her aim had gotten better because it hit me square in the head. She was pissed, but all I could do was laugh. I ain't feel bad though, not even a little. I was real glad actually.

I do not like coffee. It's bitter, and if one of them, *"I don't like how water tastes,"* muhfuckas drink it, the whole room be smelling like unwashed gym ass. Any drink that can make ya breath smell like chitlins' is an automatic no for me, but Noah loves that shit. She drinks it hot, cold, day, night. I once saw her make it with lemon and it still haunts me. I'm pretty sure her DNA is fifteen percent espresso at this point. If I got her pregnant and she had to give up coffee, I'm concerned that we'd end up on Snapped. So it was imperative that I learned how to make a good cup of it during our separation, and it was also imperative that I kept my mouth shut while she perused the aisles of Drip Drop Coffee Stop.

"What do you think of this?" she asked, showing me the salted caramel corn flavor.

Lawd, not this. Why did I have to get my woman back this way? Why did she want my opinion on this ass juice? I swallowed my irritation. I had no interest in coffee, but she asked for my opinion. For some reason she wanted it, and I wanted her.

"Personally, I think coffee beans fall out the Devil's ass crack. But you love it, and you already got a thing for caramel. Plus the salt would pair nicely with snickerdoodles or some, so I say get it."

Hey! That wasn't so bad! I gave myself a mental pat on the back for putting some effort into my answer, but then I noticed her scowl. I couldn't win for losing.

"What's up, No?" I asked.

"I want like three and it's $10 a pound," she whispered.

Now I wanted to scream. Yes, I knew Noah was broke. I heard about her losing her job when it happened, and my first instinct was to pay her high-ass rent before Nala talked me down. So I was more than happy to buy her coffee. Especially after what she did to me last night. She thinks she's blacking out during sex, but I think her brain is just blocking out the nasty shit she says to me. Last night she told me that getting to buss all on my pretty whore face made me worth the headache. Then she told me to enjoy the free beard balm.

Which I did.

One thing I knew I needed to work on when we divorced was how I talked to her. Me telling her that I ain't have to run shit by her was out of line. I knew it was cause if she had told me that, I would've imploded. There was a balance. I needed to be gentle yet firm.

"Noah, I ain't bout to play with you. Get all three and bring yo fucking ass. I got your coffee."

Welp, that failed. Fuck. I could see why last night freaked her out. What if we're just destined to keep repeating the same cycle?

I stopped my motion with a sigh. Nope, we were not repeating that shit. Noah deserved better.

"I'm sorry, Duchess," I started.

Surprisingly, she cupped my chin. Then she took the time to stroke my cheek with her thumb.

"It's ok," she whispered.

Nope. I wasn't going to let her distract me. Accountability was my new middle name.

"It ain't ok. I shouldn't talk to you like that. I just wanted to get your coffee because I know your situation, and I ain't want yo independent ass to fight me on it. But speaking to you like that ain't right."

She smiled. God, I loved seeing her smile. Then she kissed the end of my nose gently. Far too gently for me not to be in love with her. I was in love with her real bad too.

"Rudy Jones, I see you grew up," she said.

I reciprocated her nose kiss before motor boating them big ass titties of hers.

"Only in the ways that matter," I laughed.

There was only one thing I ain't like about Duchess' new shape: other folks looking at it. I think I've always been a little possessive, but I was worse after seeing the woman I was supposed to be spending the rest of my life with, wrapped up in some other nigga's arms. Technically, that was my fault, and she was single. It also ain't last very long between her and the dude, only six months. That was probably because he got that package in the mail that I sent, but I digress. The point is, I don't like sharing. I was never taught how, and it was one thing I ain't intend on learning.

So seeing this man stare my shawty down in this craft store like I wasn't standing directly behind her was blowing me. Then I felt disrespected that he even thought Noah was an option for him. Homie had on fake Jordan's with an ugly ass denim jacket. Shit had hella stains on it too. Meanwhile, Noah's pretty ass had them curls pulled off her face, showing off them high cheekbones and big eyes. Then my baby was dressed in a pretty pink turtleneck dress that hugged that ass. That ass was gone get me in trouble. Sooner rather than later too.

Sure, I could've tried to get busy with him, but my rib was still fucked up. Plus Noah would have my head for clowning in her favorite craft store. So right before he got bold enough to approach her, I got bolder. "Aye, Cher! Which one of our boys do you think would like this?" I exclaimed obnoxiously loud. "Number four?" I asked, holding up the toy with the corresponding fingers. Dirty Dan grimaced and swiveled on his heels as soon as he heard the mention of kids, and that was worth the irritated look she shot me.

"Rudy Jones, we ain't got no kids!" she whisper-yelled.

"No, not yet. You still in school. You focused on that Bible you writing and I respect that," I laughed.

A real ugly sound left her mouth while she avoided eye contact. It was the combination of laughter, a snort, and a scoff. It was also cute as fuck.

"Rude, I was gone handle it. You ain't gotta act a fool," she chided.

Duchess had a type and he wasn't it. So she probably would have shut him down smooth, but I wasn't willing to admit it right then.

"Ion know what you talking bout, Duchess," I shrugged.

She sighed before continuing down the aisle, leaving me behind. Maybe she was mad.

"You get three max. Ain't no four nobody coming outta me," she grumbled.

I smiled like the goofball I was after hearing that. Maybe we were ok. Maybe she wasn't too mad.

Noah

Confused. I was confused as hell. I've honestly been confused this whole week. Then there was yesterday. Yesterday, when we woke up together. Yesterday, when he touched me again. Yesterday, when I was scared I would lose him. He fell out in that snow and all I could think about was how cruel it'd be to have to live without Rudy Jones. Then he told me he loved me.

"I love you." He said it so naturally like he never stopped. Like we weren't hopelessly dysfunctional six years ago. He said it like he meant it, and I could tell he did. Then I had the audacity to love him back. It was truly sad, but I don't ever think I stopped loving him either. I was just tired. I was tired of pulling teeth and being the only one to fight. I knew it would never change between us. Except it had. Six years later, it had. Rudy was everything I needed him to be the first time around and that scared me. Terrified me, actually.

Why did it scare me? Intent. Did I think Rudy was manipulating me? No. It's truly not in his character. He wears his heart on his sleeve, and I knew he was up to no good as soon as I saw him in the store. He's always been that way. Upfront, not really able to hide his hand. He was intending to come here and get his wife back. He was intending to make me remember why I loved him. But all I could think about was yesterday when I almost killed him while being stupid. The way my stomach flipped seeing him laid out in that snow was treacherous. I was still madly in love with Rudolph Jones, and the thought of this not working out the second time around had me sick. Then there was the possibility that it could. It could work, we could be happy, restart together, and then we could be separated in a way that was permanent. How could I say it back knowing that those were my two options? Barely living without him, or dying to be with him. Cruel in every capacity.

If I told him that he'd likely tell me I was overthinking, and he'd be right. But taking life in strides wasn't my strong suit. Never had been. Probably why we're in the situation we're in now. With my husband, who was still very much in love with me, stuck in some weird romantic limbo. Waiting on me to tell him what I wanted. Hell, what we both wanted. Ugh. This could be so easy if I just opened my mouth. Rudy was right about one thing, I was a very unserious woman for all those fancy degrees.

"Duchess," he cooed, snapping me out of my thoughts.

"I think the graham crackers are crushed up good, Cher."

We were making a gingerbread house, and Rudy had given me a job that had absolutely nothing to do with baking. I was crushing graham crackers for texture and I still managed to fuck it up. What if I fucked us up this time around too?

"Noah, you overthinking," he sighed, sitting next to me.

Damn it. Was I really that transparent?

"About what?" I asked skeptically.

Rudy shrugged before tucking my curls behind my ears. Then he rubbed my back once he was satisfied with his view of my scrunched-up face.

"Ion know. I just know you overthinking. You wanna tell me?"

Yes, but also no. I couldn't risk giving him hope and then taking it away if I changed my mind. So I just shook my head.

"Aight, Duchess. I ain't gone push, but you gotta get out ya own head. C'mere."

He opened his arms for me and I practically fell into them, eagerly burying my head into his warm chest. He always was my safe place. Even when I was mad at him. Especially when I was frustrated with myself, and I was definitely frustrated.

"Let's roll out this cookie dough, Cher," he said, pressing behind me.

Slowly, my shoulders relaxed from my neck, settling back into their rightful place while we flattened the slab of chunky chocolate chip dough. Rudy was busy being the second coming of Richard Pryor while I tried my best not to fan his flames. The joke about ole boy's shoes was funny though. So I laughed. So he joked some more, and I laughed again. Eventually, I was clutching my belly in an attempt to catch my breath that his humor made escape me.

Then, Rudy Jones, ever the masochist, decided to hold me. He wrapped those tree trunk arms around my waist and pulled me to his chest, tucking my head underneath his chin, and I was powerless to stop him. Before I knew it, we had been dancing for an hour. No music to guide us, just the synchronized rhythm of our bodies. With Rudy's loud heartbeat calling out to mine, our bare feet gliding against the polished hardwood, and our voices humming a song that had never been written. Then, my anxiety dissolved, my pulse steadied, and I started enjoying the moment for everything it was. Happily forgetting about everything it could be.

Six

Chapter Six

Noah

You know what else was everything? Waking up wrapped in Rudolph Jones's arms. He always held me so tenderly and cradled my head and waist like I was a cherished lovie. Then the way he smelled? Lawd. Cherry wood, pine, and warm vanilla layered over oatmeal Aveeno soap. Rudy reminded me of that big bowl of Christmas potpourri my grandma had on the table from September through January. Then the man had the nerve to be warm. Here it was, twenty-eight degrees out with a hundred percent chance of snow and Rudy Jones had me sweating like we were in Aruba. But besides all that, I knew this was the safest place in the world. I was safe from all physical harm. I was safe from the pressure of reality. I was safe from myself and my rampaging thoughts of what if. As I lay tucked against my hairy naked bear on the blue light morning of December 30th, I realized what was truly important. He loved me, I loved him, and we were trying to love each other. So despite my earlier insistence that I would not fuck my ex-husband, I'm glad I did. Real glad actually.

Rudy

60

Do you know what my problem is? I sleep too heavy. I've slept through tornados, earthquakes, my mama shooting my daddy in the foot, and this morning I slept through this mischief of Noah Tyler Harrison-Jones. I ain't wake up until I heard the wind slam the door behind her like it paid bills around this bitch. Then I looked outside. It was snowing so hard I couldn't even see the chopping stump that was fifteen feet in front of my window or the truck twenty feet back. I wouldn't dare venture outside in such weather and neither should Noah. Nor was I expecting her to.

"Noah!" I hollered. "Where you coming from, girl?"

She ain't answer so I started moving around to go find out, but she appeared in my doorway just before I could get out of bed. Her arms were full of her hair products, clothes, and masturbation aides while she grinned at me.

"I'm moving in here," she announced.

Honestly, I thought that was implied since we were back on decent terms, but I was trying to keep from making assumptions. Cause I was assuming she meant for me to see that new hot pink vibrator in her hands. I was also assuming I'd put it to use later, and I was assuming I might actually have a shot with my wife.

But they say assuming make an ass out of you and me, and I really wasn't in the mood to get my heart broken for mismanaged expectations, so I decided then and there to accept whatever she was willing to give me. So as long as she kept smiling and laughing. I could be happy with that even if this week was resigned to be nothing more than a fond memory of the one that got away. I was gonna be ok with it. I had to be.

"Don't look so worried," she said, stroking my cheek. "We good, Rude."

I wanted to let my anxiety about us eat me up, but then she pressed her soft-serve body against me. My six brain cells immediately abandoned all other thoughts to focus on the chance to touch Noah, except for the one buzzkill who was telling me I needed to pee.

"I'll be back, Duchess. I need to drain the main."

She looked at me with big curious eyes before enchanting me with that pretty grin. Then I knew she was about to say some bullshit.

"Can I hold it?" she asked.

Yep, bullshit. I've never understood the fascination with women and holding dingalings, and I ain't plan on finding out either.

"Mm, no thank ya. You can hold it when I'm done. You can hold it, stroke it, s..."

She interrupted me with a loud snicker.

"Rudy Jones! Is that all you think about?" she asked.

Was it? No, of course not. But I'm not sure what else she was expecting me to think about with them big ass titties pressed against me.

"You right, I'm sorry. What I meant to say was, *"Nooooo, Duchess. Don't touch my pee pee. Girls got coochies! I'm scared of coochies!"*

She rolled her eyes at me,

"You mean cooties?" she asked.

"Nope, I mean coochies. Them hotep niggas say you attract what you fear," I shrugged.

She mushed my face while wearing that kilowatt smile, and I was glad to see it. Real glad.

You know what makes me laugh? How folks be having conversations about masculinity every sixteen seconds. Technically speaking, I was doing at least three things that should make me gay according to homophobia Twitter. I had made cinnamon rolls the night before and let them rise in the oven until this morning. I was also making cream cheese icing from scratch with my wife's pink and black Wine And Dine apron on. Yet still, there was a woman pressed against my back with her hand in my pants.

Her soft hands wrapped around my ever-hardening dick with determination. Then she stroked my shaft slowly while whispering filthy shit in my ear.

"My pussy grip tighter than this," she cooed. "I know you know."

God damn she knew how to tease a nigga. I just wanted to make breakfast and she was trying to get some milk for her coffee. I'm supposed to be the nasty one between us, but comfortable Noah? Unmatched filth.

Wait.

The realization hit me like a freight liner. She was comfortable. My wife was back comfortable with me. Fuck this was terrible. It meant if she did decide against giving me a second shot, it'd be too late for me. I'm delusional enough when she acts like she don't want me. Then this? Yeah, I was ready to start looking for jobs in New York.

Entranced. That's my new favorite word. Especially since it's the perfect phrase to describe what happens to me every time I look at Noah. My bird would call it gris gris, but either way that shortbread complexion with them deep brown eyes and pouty lips had me ready to fall at her knees. Duchess wasn't paying me no mind, though. She was too busy eating breakfast and sipping her dirty bean water. But if she licked icing off her middle finger all slow like that again, she was gone find herself impaled.

Ah, Noah. I propped my head on my hands to watch her eat. I loved watching her. I also loved being inside her. I just loved her. Dammit lawd, I was trying. I was trying to give her space and time to process her feelings, but it was taking all my willpower. I wanted to scoop her up, hold her close, and tell her she was mine and that's the end of it. I knew it wasn't right though. Duchess was her own person and I had grown past the childish shit I used to do to keep her close to me. So all I could do was wait.

And also apparently fuck. Noah was sitting on top of me licking warm icing off my rigid nipples. We ain't even make it to the bed. I honestly can't tell you how we got here. The last thing I can recall is her wiping a lil cinnamon off my bottom lip. Everything after that is a blur. Just like now. I ain't hear shit she said, I just nodded and now I'm watching her ass jiggle on my head in slow motion while she put her mouth on my other head. I could ask what was happening, but I wasn't gone question why her wet pussy was in my face. I was finna do what every self-proclaimed big boy did. I was gone eat.

"Rude," she whimpered.

I think Duchess expected me to yield once I nutted, but hearing her lucid moans when I busted in her mouth made me go harder. Her pussy was the best thing I ever tasted. Sweet like honey and slightly tangy from the release of her unrelenting orgasms. I'm sure she was ready to get up after cumming three times, but being nose deep in my wife's ass and coochie was a dream. That high-pitched squeal of hers and them claws digging into my hips was sending me to the other side. Then she creamed my face so much that I looked like I had got a hood esthetician facial. All I needed was the rose petals.

Speaking of.

"Go get your new toy, baby," I purred, withdrawing my tongue from her pearl.

I could tell Noah wanted to obey, but she was out of breath like a muhfucka. So I let her rest against my thigh while I rubbed her back, careful not to accidentally dip my finger back into her enticing box. I instead focused on the dark patch of moles covering her left hip. They patterned together to make a J shape and I always joked it was nature's tattoo for her eventual new last name. My last name. Duchess moved right as I inevitably failed to keep my fingers to myself and I called after her to make sure we ain't leave with a different kind of souvenir.

"And grab a strip of condoms, Duchess."

We definitely needed the entire strip. I had no idea how long we'd been at it, but I knew I ain't wanna stop. Especially with the way she was gushing all over me. Damn, the couch was gone need to be deep cleaned. Noah had the kind of pussy that made a nigga wanna sing gospel. Then the way she was riding me? Never mind gospel, that shit was sinful. The rhythm in her hips was the work of Lucifer Jontavious Johnson himself. I watched her whole body roll against mine in a singular, slow, and fluid movement. It felt so good my eyes rolled back into my empty ass brain. Even then she was the only thing I saw. I liked a bounce as much as the next nigga, but watching her grind on me, bucking them hips while gripping my knees, was ecstasy. Then the way her pussy clenched around me while that vibrator overstimulated her clit?

Bliss.

"Rudy, I missed this," she cried.

She was about to cum again, and her body was shaking like a stripper with no rhythm, trying to brace for it. She ain't have to tell me cause I was certain since it's all I thought about recently. Them soft ass moans, the tense eye contact we shared, Noah's vulnerability. My baby was so damn vulnerable. She was whimpering, cussing, and completely open for me. Eagerly taking whatever I threw her way, and damn was she **taking** it. I looked down and watched her pink pussy swallow my dick whole, only leaving my balls visible.

"You doing such a good job, Duchess. Look at you go, baby," I moaned deliriously.

I wasn't much of a talker when we were younger, but I needed her to know what she was doing to me. That way she might be inclined to do it again. I needed her to do it again. I then realized I spent six years craving moments like this. It's why it never worked with anyone else. I tried, but I was still hopelessly addicted to Noah Tyler Harrison-Jones.

Shit, I missed this too.

"Cmere, baby," I cooed, pulling her close.

I took over the work while she laid against my shoulder, clutching my biceps tightly, but then she closed her eyes.

That wouldn't do.

"Open your eyes, Cher. Watch me," I demanded.

Her eyelids fluttered, threatening to clamp shut again before I grabbed her chin and tilted it up.

"I said watch me, Duchess baby. I know you can do it."

So she did. She opened her eyes and those maple syrup irises of hers cast my reflection back to me while our bodies twined rhythmically. One, two. Just like my racing heart. Just like our heaving chests. Just like the syllables that had been dancing in my head since I saw her in the store.

No-ah.

Her eyes welled with tears and so did mine. I guess we're reciprocal that way. So I ain't look away even though my eyes were threatening a cry and neither did she. Cause we're reciprocal that way. She reached for me slowly, cradling my cheek in her dewy palm while I experienced the same thing she did. She was overwhelmed and so was I. I was overwhelmed and vulnerable, so my tears finally rushed down my cheeks while I buried myself inside my wife. My safe place. My everything. And when my body was busy pouring everything into her, my brain took it open itself to make my mouth do the same.

"Noah, I could never not love you. Imma always be yours," I panted.

I realized what I said the instant my dick stopped twitching and I was terrified she might stomp on my bleeding heart, but she wrapped herself around me instead.

"I guess it's one more thing we have in common, Rudy Jones," she whispered.

Noah

I woke up well past two. I couldn't remember the last time I took a midday nap, but I knew I needed it. Especially since my body felt like I'd been hit by a truck going no less than seventy miles an hour. I mean, Rudy is built like a Chevy Colorado, and he definitely ran me down so maybe it was an accurate feeling. I groaned while my muscles strained to shift. The soreness made it hard for me to even adjust my arms. It was a job for Body Armors and ibuprofen. I slowly lifted my head off my sleeping husband's chest, looking down at the mess we made. White splatters stained the cushions looking like paint instead of body fluids and cinnamon roll icing. Yeah, the couch needed to be burned. Expeditiously.

I put a blanket over Rudy after fixing myself a cure for the bangover he'd given me and got comfy at the dining room table, laptop ajar. Then I started typing. My body was worn out, but my mind was perfectly clear, allowing my ideas to flow freely. Usually, I'd be so stressed out that my thoughts were tangled like a ball of yarn, and it was impossible to pluck something out without taking everything around it. I was constantly overwhelmed and that allowed doubt to settle into the cracks of my mind, but it was absent after a few days of dealing with Rudy Jones. *"You are so smart,"* he said. Four little words made everything clear. I could focus, I could write, and then eventually, I was finished.

I had finished my dissertation. It had taken me ten months of sobbing, struggling, and sleeplessness in the name of research, and I struggled to push through to the end. Then I spent one week with Rudolph Jeremiah Jones. What had he done to me that I couldn't do for myself? I wracked my mind for an answer while tracing the shape of my nails, then it hit me. He balanced me. He poured into me, made me have some fun and *sleep,* and I was better for it. I was better for him. I was better with him. Tears rolled down my cheeks while I peered around the corner at the bear hibernating peacefully on the couch. I realized I still needed him. Probably always would.

One thing that always concerned me about Rudy was how heavy he slept. Armageddon could be happening in the front yard and he'd snooze right on through it. I had fried chicken, mashed potatoes, and even successfully avoided burning a pan of cornbread. I mean, it was Jiffy mix, but it was cornbread! I lifted the lid off my green beans to add the balsamic and gave them a quick stir, nothin was better than fresh green beans sauteed with garlic. My shoulders relaxed while I poured my tart glaze over them, making me realize how much I missed cooking.

New York was high as hell, so the same green beans would have cost me $3 more. Then I was busy as hell. When I was working I'd start my day at five. Leave the house at six, get to work by seven, work until five thirty, get back home at seven, clean, shower, write, and then just barely scarf down Lean Cuisine. I promised myself I'd take a break or find some sort of balance, but I never did. Until now that is.

"You cooked," Rudy said, wrapping his arms around me.

"Thank you, Duchess. I'll make the plates."

I gasped because I ain't even hear him get up. He moves way too quietly to be that big.

"I ain't mean to scare you," he chuckled.

I padded over to him and face-planted onto his chest.

"You need a bell," I mumbled.

"Is that a sex thing?" he laughed.

Even though I felt how Debo likely felt after getting smacked with a brick, I immediately took delight in the visualization of Rudy in a strappy leather harness with a bell hanging around his neck. I let my hands roam the expanse of his back before curling my fingers into his waistband, but he stopped me with unfortunate news.

"Ou, I'm so sorry, Duchess. I ain't got nothin' for you for the rest of today. My balls hurt from you bouncing on my shit."

Tch. After all these years I finally wore Rudy Jones out? Unbelievable.

"You getting old," I sighed.

Rudy snapped his head back in disbelief that I could say such a thing.

"Ain't you 30?" he asked.

"What that got to do with anything? You the one that tapped out," I shrugged.

Rudy sat the plates down and his lips curled into an irritated smirk. I didn't know if he wanted to laugh or dump me in the snow, but he pulled out my chair so I guessed I was momentarily safe.

"Yo lil nasty ass tryna touch me when you should be writing that dissection," he chided.

I sat, letting the big man push me in and get back to his chair before telling him the good news.

"I actually finished my dissertation earlier. So this is kinda like a celebration lunch."

Rudy dropped his fork and met my gaze. His mouth hung open slightly while he rubbed his thumb and pointer finger together. Then he spoke.

"Duchess, you finished your paper?" he asked.

I nodded just long enough to miss him scrambling out of his seat to come kiss all over me.

"I'm so so proud of you," he whispered.

I reveled in the kisses placed on my cheeks and forehead before he finally arrived at my lips. Rudy hesitated for a second, likely because the last lip lock we shared caused some awkwardness, but I leaned in first, accepting whatever was to come. Damn, Rudy Jones was a good kisser. So good that I completely forgot that we were eating lunch, celebrating my paper, and properly divorced. Cause in that moment, all I could think about was how right his lips felt on mine, and how getting to celebrate every milestone like this would be a dream.

We also celebrated by building snowmen after lunch. Rudy insisted that I enjoy something creative after using most of my brain power for my dissertation for three months. Plus we needed to walk off the gravy. So there I was at the big age of thirty, packing snow to make a party hat. Or at least I thought I was.

"What is that?" Rudy asked.

"A hat," I clicked.

I watched him suspiciously tilt his head onto his shoulder before shrugging.

"Yo snowman a lame, my homie getting a snapback."

I stood there, mouth open, fist curled, while he chuckled. Then I stomped through the crunchy, frozen snow and knocked his snowman's head off.

"Now who snowman a lame?" I spat.

I celebrated my victory prematurely, laughing at the disbelief plastered all over his usually smug face. Then I felt an arm lift underneath my waist and another on my knees.

"Rudy Jones! Don't you dare!" I fussed.

It was too late, he threw me in the snow. My body sank into the frigid embankment quickly, leaving me no time to scramble out before it could wet my hair. My hair that I spent an hour on yesterday. I was gonna kill that man. He started to run when I finally freed myself, but hell hath no fury like a twist-out ruined. So I scooped up as much snow as my hands could hold, packed it tight, cocked my arm back, and threw my weight into it. My snowball soared spectacularly, hitting him right in the neck, and making him wince. I was satisfied and I started to walk back inside. Rudy Jones, however, was not.

I hardly heard him pace back across the yard before I felt strong hands tug me away from the door.

"Not so fast, Duchess," he laughed. "You can dish it but you can't take it?"

Technically he was right. Technically I had started it by violating his snowman, but he called my snowman a lame. My actions were wholly justified.

"You gone beat up on some poor defenseless woman?" I gasped, trying to wiggle out of his hold.

"You hardly defenseless the way you just pegged my ass, Cher," he laughed.

I didn't have a good rebuttal so I chose to fall limp in his arms instead. I once again hoped that the giant was feeling gentle enough to take pity on me, and I was rewarded with Rudy's light chuckle.

"You unbelievable, Duchess. Come on, let's go back in. My side hurting."

I immediately broke free of his hold. For all the playing and, uh *playing* we had done, I forgot Rudy was still recovering. Recovering from a bruised rib after a brush with death at that.

"Rudolph Jones! The doctor said no lifting and strenuous activity and you out here picking me up! You so d..."

Rudy

Noah chewed my ass out for about fifteen minutes before she finally ran out of wind. I ain't think she ever would after ten minutes. My baby would have public speaking on lock if she wasn't so damn anxious. She passed me two ibuprofen and a cold Body Armor with a scowl, and I couldn't help but chuckle. It was the same stank eye she shot me before giving me some ass, so I was feeling lucky.

"Ain't shit funny," she fussed.

"A nigga can't smile at yo pretty ass?" I mused.

She rolled her eyes before motioning me to take my meds, and she skirted away once satisfied. I knew I was tap dancing on her nerves but I couldn't help myself, so I followed after her on my bullshit.

"No, baby. You against smiling now?" I asked.

Noah spun around and I twisted with her to hold her hand, but I doubled over as aching pain spread across my chest and midsection. I half expected another scowl following a well-deserved *I told you so*, but Noah instead guided me to the couch that wasn't desecrated.

"Lay back," she commanded.

I wanted to fight and assure her I had it handled, but the pain in a nigga chest was literally screaming otherwise. So I got comfortable while she took off all my snow gear. She moved through my clothes so quick that you woulda thought I offered her some dick, and I was impressed until she got to my beanie. She crouched down and slowly curled her fingers under the knitted band to slip my hat off, taking the time to scratch my curly new growth after she did. God, her little fingers felt so good in my scalp. Like a rattail comb getting the itchy spots. But if the pain ain't knock the wind out of me, the way Noah was staring at me would've. Her big eyes absorbed the last trickling sunlight, making them shine amber instead of their usual maple, and I was drowning in shawty shit. I could see the kids, the holidays with Nala, the nasty-ass cornbread, and the rest of our days. I could see everything in her because she was everything. Her pupils blew wide as she leaned closer to take me all in and I guess she could see the same things. Eventually, our noses touched, prompting Noah to plant a little kiss on the end of mine, and I whimpered. I whimpered like a punk bitch, but I ain't regret it. I was glad for it actually. Real glad.

We spent the rest of the day watching Christmas movies after Noah got me familiar with a heating pad. I ain't gone lie, that thang was pressure. I saw why that muhfucka was basically her man when she was on. Shit had me so relaxed I thought I was high. She put on the next installment of Home Alone before snuggling back onto my chest and I don't think I've ever been that peaceful. There was a soft lady on my body, my stomach was full, and the night was quiet. I could've fallen asleep if Noah ain't break me from my trance.

"I wish I did this on Christmas," she sighed.

That had me concerned. I was a Grinch once upon a time, but Noah and Big Noah always did it up for the holidays. Big, stupid-ass trees, twinkling light displays, festive drinks with way too much cinnamon on rotation, loads of gifts, and even caroling. Before Noah, I ain't know not nan Black folk who was going around caroling. Shit, the only Black folk I expected to be knocking on doors was Jehovah's Witnesses and repo men.

"Whatchu do for Christmas?" I asked skeptically. Noah had gotten to Heaven's Peak on the twenty-sixth, and long boring-ass flight aside, I knew she ain't spend Christmas morning traveling too.

"Not much, I ended up doing some side gigs. I did get a cup of hot chocolate though," she yawned.

The vision of a worn-out Noah sitting alone in her shitty-ass shoebox apartment with only a cup of hot chocolate to keep her company broke my heart. Especially considering how hard she used to work to make the holidays special for me.

"No, you worked, baby?" I gasped.

"Yes, Rude. I gotta pay rent in two days like the rest of the normies," she sneered.

She had a lil attitude, but I was gone let it slide cause I knew she was just stressed and depressed. Noah thrived under stability and her life was chaotic as fuck lately. Which made me determined to pay her rent whether or not my week of scheming worked out.

"Next year is gone be better, Cher. You'll be finished with school, with a fire-ass job. Hopefully outta that raggedy ass apartment, an…"

I was trying to be affirming but she interrupted me with a question I ain't see coming.

"I'll have Rudy Jones by my side?" she asked.

Remember what I said about assuming? Yeah, she was making it hard. Real hard. But I still tried not to get too ahead of myself even though all her flags were coming up green. Managing expectations of others was a big topic for me in therapy, and I ain't spending all that money talking to that lady for fun.

"Yeah, if you want. I'll be wherever you want me to be, Cher."

She nuzzled my neck with that lil box nose and my spine tingled from the sensation of her warm peppermint breath on my skin. The shit was so magical I was uncomfortable, so I had to crack a joke to ease it.

"Especially if you want me between them cheeks, baby."

She popped me on the arm before her withheld laughter tickled my skin some more, making me drowsy from happiness.

"Stop talking, Rudy Jones," she snickered.

I usually wasn't one to make demands to but for Noah? Yeah, I'll shut the fuck up.

Chapter Seven

R
udy

I woke up in a panic. It had only been a couple of days since Noah started sleeping with me, but feeling her absence in my morning haze was jarring as fuck. So when I swept the bed and she wasn't there, I sat straight up, hoping she ain't run her lil ass back out there in a snowstorm.

"Noah, where you at?" I hollered.

I heard some shuffling before a light voice sang back, "In the living room!"

"Doing what?" I asked suspiciously.

I heard something else crinkle before she shot back,

"Minding mine!"

I narrowed my eyes while staring out in the hall. Was Noah testing me? Probably. Was I about to get my ass outta bed and fall into her trap anyway? Yes, yes I was.

I was surprised to see my robe had been snatched from me, and I walked into the front room in just boxers to express my irritation with that fact. But I had to pause when I rounded the corner because the sight of Noah had a nigga ready to cry.

"Happy Birthday, Rude!" she shouted.

I sucked in a breath while looking around the room. Golden balloons trimmed with white and green ribbon filled the space. Sunlight flooded the room and danced across a few elaborately wrapped gifts to the left, a modest French toast station was to my right, and Noah stood in the center in my robe with some lacy-ass emerald green lingerie, holding a golden thirty-one balloon. Yeah, my next trip around the sun was off to a good start. A great start even.

"When did you get all of this?" I asked while gnawing on some pepper bacon.

"Yesterday when you heard me come back in. I drove down to Aspen," she replied.

Aspen is an hour and a half away from Heaven's Peak. So that meant Noah was up before the sun to take her trip and get back here before 10:30. Which made this very intentional. I think I liked intention on her.

"Duchess, you ain't have to do this for my birthday," I started.

She quieted me by shoving a sugar plum in my mouth,

"You right, but I did. So hush and enjoy your 31st, Rudy Jones."

I chewed the unrequested fruit solemnly while she chuckled at my expression. Then my phone rang.

"Happy birthday, Rude!" Nala cheered. "What you...ope."

Nala snatched her hands back while I fumbled to switch the camera back to my face instead of a departing, lingerie-wrapped, Noah. As much as me and her auntie talked, I hadn't exactly been honest about my plot to reclaim my wife. I was tryna do a soft launch or whatever the fuck them people call it.

"Okay, then! You went and got yo woman back! That's my real nephew!" she cheered.

Noah scurried away all red in the face while I tried to shoot Nala the look, but as she told me before, she was too old to give a damn.

"Tuh! Y'all too grown to be embarrassed! I really ain't even think this divorce bullshit would last this long," she shrugged.

I pinched the bridge of my nose. Nala always chose violence. This was exactly why my wife acted the way she did, asking doctors if she could fuck me in the middle of a diagnosis.

But I wasn't tryna get ahead of myself, Nala approval or not.

"It ain't like that, Auntie. We just friendly," I sighed.

"Yeah, y'all real friendly. Friendly as hell the way Noah got them big ass titties out," she laughed.

Me and Duchess both groaned while Nala cackled menacingly. I remember when I was seventeen and Charlene caught me sucking Noah's pussy in the driveway, I thought that was bad, but somehow this felt worse.

"Uh, I gotta go," I gasped, unable to think of a good excuse.

Nala shrugged before ultimately dismissing me, but not before leaving me with one last comment.

"Gone head enjoy your birthday, Rude. I was just calling to say, hi. But don't let your New Year's Resolution become baby proofing yo house," she winked. "Tell Noah I said I love her."

She hung up and left me covering my mouth in shock while Noah walked back in fully dressed.

"Nala sends her love," I mumbled.

I don't like birthdays. I never have, and I probably never would if not for Noah. I honestly didn't celebrate them until we were 16. Most times my folks was too fucked up to even acknowledge my birthday, so gifts and celebrations were out of the question. Then Noah's lil ass came along, demanding that I be treated like a human being and shit. For my 16th birthday, she got me a phone that wasn't held together by duct tape. It was a Sidekick. Every key was functional, and the muhfucka had a camera. So that year I learned that I really liked photography, and also birthdays, and of course, Noah. Then this year was no different.

"Where the fuck you get this from?" I asked.

I was staring at the lens of a nearly mint condition Polaroid 600 Supercolor. It had been on my wish list for years, but I was always outbid or too slow to discover the listing.

"I know a guy," she shrugged.

My jealous heart ain't like that answer too much, and I guess she could tell because she laughed at my mean mug.

"Not that type of guy, Rude. Not every nigga wants me."

Everything in me was screaming; I WANT YOU! ME! I DO! But I reeled that shit in an effort not to get my feelings hurt on my birthday. I still ain't know if the feeling was truly mutual. She always joked and said I had a permanent spot on her roster no matter what we had going on, so maybe she was just keeping true to that. I was ready to get lost in my thoughts, but then Noah went and pressed those soft lips on my forehead. A nigga really was simple cause that was all I needed to be completely rerouted.

"Aight, Rudy Jones. Two more."

I opened the smaller box first, revealing a crocheted beanie big enough for my locs. It was green and satin lined, and it was woven with a fire-ass star point pattern. I only ever knew one woman who crocheted star point patterns. My wife.

"Noah, when did you get the time to do this?" I asked.

I saw her pick up yarn at the craft store, but I ain't think nothing of it. Noah had a yarn habit like niggas had shoe habits. It was a given at this point.

"Last night. You really do sleep heavy, Rude," she laughed.

"I know, I know. But you did this fast as fuck, shawty," I noted, looking over the solid construction.

"It's just a hat, Rude," she said dismissively. "I was originally aiming for a blanket or gloves."

I rolled my eyes and pushed her over. She always thought she could do better, but I was satisfied with my hat. Especially when I put it on and it fit over my ears.

I didn't tell Noah that though, I just went quiet. Which in hindsight probably wasn't the best idea, because when I finally did react, I freaked her anxious ass out. She yelped when I slung her over my shoulder and spun around with her.

"YOU MADE ME A HAT!" I hollered excitedly.

"Rudy Jones! Put me down!" she cried.

I was having too much fun to stop until my rib started hurting again, and then I yielded in the interest of self-preservation. She watched me hobble towards the clean couch with crossed arms and another scowl.

"Fucked yourself up again?" she asked.

"Yeah," I groaned.

"Jesus, Rude. You stressful," she mumbled, walking off.

Noah eventually returned with *our* heating pad and my third and final gift. It was the smallest of them all, and it wasn't wrapped like the other two. It was in a lil gift baggie with gold, green, and black tissue paper sticking out the top.

"Wait, close your eyes!" Noah demanded.

"Close my eyes?" I asked.

"Yes, Rude. Close your eyes and reach in."

I stared at her for a second, wondering what could be inside that I needed to close my eyes for. I wasn't a fan of going into stuff blindly, gifts or not, and Noah knew that.

"You trust me?" she asked.

I did. I trusted her with my life. Literally. So I closed my eyes, stuck my hand out, and waited for the telling sound of crinkled paper before my fingers came into contact with something soft. Something *fuzzy.*

I wrapped my hand around the velvety object and pulled it out, opening my eyes to reveal a black cat Beanie Baby, with a makeshift *Harley* name tag. I looked up at Duchess and tears was spilling out my sensitive ass before the words could. But when they did come, it was a bunch of unintelligible gibberish.

"You… you. Thi… this," I stammered.

Noah ain't reply, she just leaned forward to kiss my tears away. It was funny how a simple $6 gesture could bring me to tears. It was funny how I told

Noah that story once when we were drunk off our asses ten years ago and she remembered. It was funny how my heart was skipping beats even though the doctor said it was perfectly fine at the ER, and it was funny how this was somehow my best birthday yet. Even with my wife who was technically and legally, not my wife, begrudgingly spending the week with me. Yeah, life was funny. Real funny.

Noah

I was grateful for Rudy's initial boundary with the master's bedroom. Even though it had recently been brought to my attention that he never planned for us to be in separate beds for long. Damn, his type-A personality. But still, I appreciated the thought, because the master bedroom was made for romance. The plush down-bed stretched across the entire right wall, to the left sat a jetted hot tub, and in front of that, there was a big bay window overlooking the valley. I could stare out that window all day, and I had before, yet I had no plans to do that this time.

Rudy Jones had turned thirty-one and I was here to celebrate it. So I used everything in my under-funded, but crafty arsenal to celebrate him. That included filling this hot tub with his favorite milk bath and finding as many half-burned three wicks as I could to create a candlelit ambiance. I thought he would ruin my surprise, but he was busy doing something in the kitchen and he told me to beat it. I would've been upset if not for my own ulterior motives. Plus he was making cornbread, and we both deserved good cornbread after enduring my plate of sand. Shit was dry as hell. So, so dry.

But eventually, Rudy came looking for me. I figured he would. I was quiet and he once said a quiet Noah was an overthinking Noah. Technically he wasn't wrong, but this time I wasn't overthinking. I was daydreaming. I don't know why, but the color of the bath sent me straight back into a vision of the other day on the couch. Actually, I do know why. I know exactly why, and I was hoping Rudy Jones might remind me later.

"Duchess," he cooed, motioning to the room. "What's this, baby?"

"Birthday bath," I said, swinging my arm.

I thought he'd get naked immediately, but he instead stood perfectly still, staring at me like I grew a second head.

"Duchess."

"Rude."

He mumbled something under his breath while walking towards me. Then he pinched the bridge of his nose. Did I scare him off? Was I coming on too strong? Did I get this wrong? Was this whole thing just about sex? I had more nonsensical questions swishing around in my brain but Rudy pulled the plug on them by kissing me. God, his lips on mine felt so right. So tender, so eager, so deserving. So Rudy Jones.

My heart was racing like an office worker after five. So I deepened the kiss, sucking his bottom lip in my mouth like my life depended on it. I guess I was doing too much cause Rudy eventually had to pull away to catch his breath. I was honestly fine with drowning in him until he so rudely reminded me we needed air. But our current situation wasn't unpleasant either. Rudy bent slightly to press his forehead to mine, allowing me to smell the honey and lemon on his breath from a hot toddy. It mixed perfectly with his natural scent to send me into a dazed frenzy. God, I was hopeless.

I expected him to make a move once he caught his breath, but he hadn't. He stood perfectly still until those intense brown eyes flickered to meet my gaze. Just like the window, I could spend hours getting lost in Rudolph Jones's eyes. His lips never parted, but the need that swirled in his dilated pupils told me just how much he missed me these last few years. So I watched myself in his careful gaze. I was new and raw and so desperately in need of him, and I knew he could tell.

So I got bold and met Rudy's mouth, stopping just short of bridging the divide between us. Then I let my bottom lip slowly graze his, and I took the time to let myself enjoy the electricity racing down my spine and settling into my fingertips. I took the time to savor every groove and ridge of Rudy's lips, and I took the time to see the man in front of me. The one who never stopped loving me, even when he probably should have.

He collected a few curls hanging in my eyes and carefully brushed them behind my ear to get a better look at me. Then I watched those wonderfully thick lips curl into an anxious grin.

"You ain't have to do all this, Duchess," he repeated.

"I wanted to," I sighed. "Make up for the last six I missed."

Rudy's eyes started to water, and I was prepared to dry his tears, but he instead sucked in a sharp breath before kissing the top of my head.

"I don't deserve you," he sniffled.

I remember saying that to hurt him in an argument once, but it couldn't have been farther from the truth. Rudy deserved so much more than the mess life threw at his feet. He deserved celebration, kindness, and consideration. He deserved happiness, love, and compassion. Then, here and now, he deserved everything I had to give him. Even with the IOU in my bank account and my very palpable fear that this could go wrong. But if Rudy Jones could meet me where I was, I could do the same for him. So I did.

I didn't respond audibly, I just shook my head and slipped off his robe before guiding him to the tub. He eased into the torrid water slowly, spreading his thick legs to give me space to fit between them. For some reason, I was nervous. Maybe it was because I was closer to a decision. Maybe it was because we left the next day. Or maybe it was the way Rudy Jones was staring at me. Like I was the punishment and the cure. Heaven, hell, and everything in between. Or the answer to one of life's most daunting questions. I somehow felt more exposed than usual while standing in front of him, but I didn't dare break our gaze. I just focused on those exigent earthen eyes, and I was face-to-face with him before I could even realize I got in the tub.

We watched each other in silence for a few minutes, with the occasional sizzling of a burning wick narrating our peace. To tell the truth, I was never good with eye contact, but with Rudy? It was akin to the gift of a thousand engaging conversations, a hundred melodic songs, and infinite moments of shared hilarity all without ever saying an audible word. It was nothing short of perfect. I wished I could be immortalized in his gaze sometimes. However, Rudy eventually shifted, and I noticed his arm slowly rise from the creamy bath to meet the back of my neck. His hand braced my nape and crown while his fingers combed through my wild curls, gathering a few to hold while he did so. He tilted my head back to expose my neck, and his lips hovered against my horripilated skin, teasing a kiss.

"You know why I like winter so much, Duchess?" he asked.

I never knew for sure why Rudy Jones loved winter, but I had a few ideas.

"Cause bears get to hibernate in the winter?" I replied.

"No," he mumbled, grazing my throat.

"Oh, cause of the holidays?"

"No," he whispered, nipping my ear.

I was running out of guesses, and since his lips were on my body, I was running out of brainpower. I knew it wasn't his birthday because he hardly wanted to celebrate it most years. I knew it wasn't snow, cause he always cursed about having to drive on icy roads with idiotic assholes, and I knew it wasn't cause of our annual cabin trip either, seeing as we were just coming off a six-year hiatus.

"Tell me," I panted breathlessly. "Is it warm drinks?"

Rudy chuckled before sinking his sharp white canines into my collar. Me and the candle wax became one and the same. Molten, hot, and burning for Rudy Jones. But he pulled away from me before I got too dazed, seemingly interested in answering my earlier question. His eyes drew mine back into our vortex before he parted his plush lips to speak, and I was wholly unprepared for his answer.

"Because of you," he confessed. "Because you hate the cold, so you extra cuddly. Because back then, you stopped counting calories in the winter, and I was happy to witness your little sugar highs. And because I can see the goosebumps on your skin when you chilly, or excited, or nervous, and all I want to do is kiss every single one. So I like winter so much because I like you. Actually, I love you. Real bad," he said matter of factly.

Funny, my last guess would have been something about the promise of a New Year's resolution, but I liked his actual answer better. I liked it so much that my usually overactive brain turned off. Then I pressed my mouth to his.

Rudy's tension melted away when we parted our lips to deepen the kiss. I felt his shoulders relax before he pulled me closer into his embrace, closer to his heart. I was spinning like always, lost in his signature scent, intoxicating kisses, and strong arms. A thousand auric sunny days without him would never compare to a singular overcast day spent being in his arms. And I know because I lived it. I had lived without the jokes, the scalp scratches, and the pep talks. All in an effort to live without frustration and fears, but it honestly never felt worth the trade. I pulled away to look into his eyes, finally understanding why he was staring at me so hard the entire week. Rudolph Jones was my curse, cure, heaven, and hell. Rudy Jones was my everything.

My swollen lips parted before my brain could weigh the pros and cons of my following statement. I guess my body was fed up with my brain's need for control and logic since every cell in me was screaming the same thing.

"I love you, Rudolph Jones," I mumbled.

Rudy's pupils dilated while he nibbled on that thick bottom lip, and then his mouth darted into an anxious smile.

"Yeah?" he asked.

I nodded, clearing a few fallen locs from his face.

"Yeah, real bad," I whispered.

I can't tell you the last time I made out with someone as an adult. I think it had been at least four years, and it wasn't even that great. Too many grown people suck at kissing, and not in a good way. Then there was Rudy Jones. He held my neck and back while our mouths thrashed together, leaving me completely breathless. He was eager, but his kisses were still tender and careful. From the way he nibbled and sucked on my bottom lip, to the way he licked the roof of my mouth, and especially the way his tongue twisted around mine. It was like a snake enveloping its prey, and I had fallen head-first into his trap. I wanted to slow down, but his heavy hands flexed in an attempt to keep me as close as possible while his third leg cheered me on from the bleachers. Then he tasted so fucking good like heirloom tea, lemons, and farmer's market honey. He pulled me further into his lap while I clung to his shoulder blades and I instantly knew. I was as good as gone fucking with Rudy Jones.

"Duchess… Wait, baby," he groaned.

I suspended my hips while squatting over Rude's continuously impressive erection. He was literally seconds away from the ride of his life, but for some reason, he stopped me. I just hoped it was for good reason, Agnes had gotten over purring and she was practically growling at him.

"Yes, Rude?" I asked sweetly.

Rudy gave me a little grin while clearing the rogue curls out of my eyes. He was so sweet and thoughtful that I really couldn't be too frustrated. I was just hoping he wanted to Christen our reunion in the big bed.

"We need to eat dinner," he chuckled.

I was appalled, shocked, flabbergasted, confounded even. He stopped me from sitting on it for two slices of cornbread and cabbage? Nah.

"Dinner, nigga?" I shot back.

He nodded with that same bright smirk before rubbing my nose with his.

"Dinner, Duchess."

I enjoyed the sweet touch, but I pulled back to make sure my scowl was effective.

"Respectfully, Rude, I don't give two fucks about dinner. Dinner can wait. I'm sure we'll work up a bigger appetite anyway," I said, realigning my hips.

Unfortunately, Rudy paused my motion by holding me in place, silently insistent that we take a break.

"Ugh! Fine! I guess we'll eat since you in the mood for greens over pussy!" I hollered.

Rudy popped me on my ass, making the water ripple as I attempted to climb out of the tub.

"Yeah aight, Cher. That bratty ass attitude gone get you folded like a towel, you keep it up."

I huffed and griped but I was really smiling inside. Rudy Jones wasn't the only one capable of plotting.

I was shocked to find a robe with my initials on it waiting in the living room. I guess Rudy got tired of me stealing his, but I wasn't mad at it. It was pink and equally as plush as his, with a satin-trimmed hoodie, and an optional zipper to keep my titties under control. I would question why it was so perfect if I wasn't in the middle of trying to fuck his brains out, but I decided to sit at the kitchen table and wait on my dinner instead.

It didn't take long though. Rudy emerged from the kitchen carrying two cloched plates about five minutes after leaving me high and undry.

"You are so dramatic," I said, motioning to the steel covers.

Rudy flashed me that megawatt smile before shrugging at my remark.

"Yes, yes I am. And you like it," he replied.

"Sometimes," I shrugged. "Sometimes you aight."

He spread his brows apart while nodding in acknowledgment.

"Just aight, Duchess?" he asked.

I shrugged again, clearly provoking him to choose violence.

"I wasn't just aight the other day when I was turning you inside out. According to you, I was a fine-ass menace with a big, perfect dick," he mumbled, leaning close to my parted lips.

"Ain't that what you said?" he asked, urging me to speak with his hand against my throat.

I was back in his gaze. This time my reflection flickered with the warm orange light being generated by the fireplace. He poured me a drink with those bright cognac eyes, encouraging me to sip until I forgot what was left and right. So I did. I drank in his demanding gaze, the feel of his calloused hands gently squeezing my soft windpipe, and his moisturized merlot skin that shined like polished gold. Then I was drunk before I knew it, and I was threatening to get belligerent.

"Rudolph Jones," I started. "If you don't let go of me within the next fifteen seconds, I'm gone knock this shit on the floor and do something to you."

Rudy's eyes withdrew from mine, breaking the spell he had me under before we both ended up with mashed potatoes stuck to our ass. He sat still for a while, seemingly calming himself from doing something reckless, and all I wanted to do was egg him on. But he eventually looked back up at me with a softer expression and a chuckle.

"You gone get me in serious trouble, Duchess," he laughed.

I probably was, because thirty minutes ago I practically said, *"Condom? We don't know her."* To be fair, I was more than sure I was good to go, and Rudy had eagerly provided me with his clean bill of health when I first agreed to let him have his way with me. So really, the only thing to worry about was the very limited potential for pregnancy, and I wasn't concerned with that either since my period was three days away and I had an IUD. So I was still thinking about ways to get filled like a Twinkie and stuffed like a turkey before Rudy redirected my attention.

"Cher, there's plenty of time for you to make me blush later. Focus on the task at hand, baby."

I sighed before I realized Rudy said I made him blush. Who would have thought that I could turn out nasty-ass Rudy Jones?

But I was trying to focus on the task at hand, so I diverted my gaze from his crotch to the gleaming silver covers that Rudy had his hands on. I leaned forward in an effort to get a little sniff and figure out why he was so excited, but all I really knew was that we were eating something savory. The scent of garlic, onion, and cooked peppers flooded my nose, making my mouth water and my stomach growl audibly.

"Mm, and you said you wasn't hungry," he mumbled.

He was being a smug know-it-all, but the food smelled good so I let him have it. Besides, I technically never said I wasn't hungry. I was just hungry for dick first and foremost.

The cloches lifted and I nearly cried when he scooted my plate toward me. Why? The food was pretty typical New Year's grub. Stewed cabbage with sausage and onions, golden cornbread glistening with honey and butter, and pot roast. But then I noticed a bowl of bright yellow mustard and sugar black-eyed peas. The same black-eyed peas that my daddy made every single New Year's Eve to protect us and bring us prosperity. The same black-eyed peas that I never learned how to make.

"Rude," I started. "Is this?"

Rudy tucked his lips inward for safekeeping so he could focus on consoling me. Then he nodded while clearing my curls from my eyes.

"Yeah, I found Senior's recipe box in the attic a few years back. I wanted to reach out and tell you, but I guess some of the food made me feel close to you."

He held my hand while easing the wrapped recipe box across the table. It was small and wooden, originally belonging to my grandmother, and although it had been polished, the sixty-year container still displayed its most cherished feature. Deep scratches from years of love, use, and migration. Including one from when I accidentally knocked it off the counter after catching the stove on fire with a burnt pie. Bless my daddy's heart for trying, but I was truly a hopeless baker. I guess that's what I had Rudy Jones for though.

"Rudy, I can't believe you kept this," I mumbled.

"Please don't be mad, Duchess. I ain't keep it to be evil," he whispered.

Now that I knew. Anybody else would have said fuck my lil raggedy recipes and tossed my shit in the trash right with the junk mail, but not Rudy Jones. He had not only kept it, but restored it, and even practiced recipes out of it. Then he had brought it to me, not truly knowing if I would stay or leave.

"I'm not," I said, choking on my salty tears. "I just... I really don't know what to say. This is the most thoughtful thing anyone's ever done for me," I whispered.

It was true. My uncle Nick had done a fine job of trashing most of my daddy's belongings so he could sell the house, and the only things I really had left of him were the cabin, an old pair of black leather oxford dress shoes, and now the box. *"And Rudy."* I thought. Senior had always reminded me I picked well even when I was fed up and frustrated, and now I had the living proof sitting across from me with a plate of peas. I teared up remembering his wedding speech about how he always wanted a son and how he was double blessed to get Rudy. Maybe the past wasn't all bad. I had been feeling stuck lately anyway, so maybe going back was helping me move forward. Life could be funny that way. Real funny.

Chapter Eight

Noah

"Thank you, Duchess," Rudy cooed.

I hummed back before dipping my finger into the dwindling jar of Blue Magic to scoop up the last few bits. Then I flattened the pad of my pointer finger against Rudy's scalp to oil his last few parts. His hair was growing fast. It was already chin-length and he had just started his locs back in January. He thought they were still in the awkward phase, but I disagreed. His thick hair framed his pointed ears and high cheekbones perfectly, especially when he smiled. He passed me my tea mug and a wipe for my hands when I finished. It was a little over an hour until midnight and we were sitting in front of the fireplace sharing the big rocker while watching The Times Square chaos on TV. I was honestly glad to be avoiding it that year, especially given my current alternative.

The peas were good. They tasted just like Seniors, and I was able to enjoy the rest of the meal once I stopped crying. Rudy had become quite the cook these last few years, and I could easily see myself gaining happy weight if I continued on. The velvety robe clung to my curves while the momentum from the swing of the chair pushed my bosom forward, making my nipples hard from the slight brush from the soft fabric. Then Rudy Jones was back to staring at me. He was wide-eyed with a calm smile that told me exactly how he was planning on bringing in the New Year. Rudy Jones was planning on bringing in the New Year with a bang.

I kneeled before him on the warm mosaic tile trimming the hearth, slowly unzipping my robe while a quiet Rudy Jones watched keenly. My breast fell free, resting against my stomach while I stared back. Then, just before I could make my next move, Rudy leaned forward and placed his thumb against my tongue and bottom lip, urging me to suck while he kneaded my breast. His gaze was tight and demanding, so I did. I sucked his thumb while his free hand roamed my body. Kneading, caressing, and tracing. He paid equal attention to my breast, tummy, and thighs before he commanded me to spread my legs, then his hand cupped my pussy while two of his fingers stretched me open. He let his thumb circle my hard clit while I ground against him like a feral cat in heat. The room was mostly silent except for the crackling of the fireplace and my lucid moans, but that didn't deter me. I could tell Rudy was enjoying himself from the way he bit his bottom lip while I squeezed around his fingers. Then again, Rudy was a sadist, so my torture was his delight.

Rudy continued to overwhelm me with his hands until I eventually squirted into his palm. I had completely unraveled, moaning so loud that it made my throat hoarse. He smiled while I caught my breath, and then that smile turned into a devilishly depraved chuckle when he leaned back to unfasten his robe. I was still kneeling before him, still catching my breath while those brown eyes of his pierced me. He looked down at his lap, then back up at me, urging me to follow his sightline. I did as I was told and I was rewarded with a show. Rudy once again used my essence to stroke his dick. I watched him, completely mesmerized while his grip tightened around his shaft and pointed his head in my direction. My breath hitched involuntarily when I heard a grunt escape his beckoning lips, then Rudy smiled before stopping. I should have been concerned, but I was too entranced to notice how dark his eyes got.

He leaned forward slowly before hooking his hands underneath my arms and dragging me forward. Then he pressed his thumb against my lower lip again.

"Open," he barked.

I felt like being difficult so I stuck my tongue out before snapping my jaw shut, but Rudy was patient. His mouth darted into a delusional grin before he wrapped his hand in my thick hair and tilted my head upward. He then put the two fingers he fucked me with inside my mouth, gently pressing my tongue downward before he not-so-gently asked again.

"Op-en," he said, stretching the syllables.

I figured I should probably listen since his other three fingers were squeezing my throat. So I opened my mouth wide, letting my tongue rest against the top of my chin. Rudy withdrew his fingers from me to guide my waiting mouth to his hard dick. I could still smell myself on his skin, and it distracted me until I snapped back to reality with his next command.

"Suck," he instructed.

I could have argued or snatched back, but I had been literally dreaming about getting my face fucked since I saw him in the store. So I slowly descended his length, desperately trying my hardest to swallow the tree trunk he called a dick. It was hard at first, but I was good once I remembered to breathe through my nose. I then picked up my pace, bobbed furiously, and ran my tongue against his frenum as I sucked, all while digging my nails into his hips. I was in heaven, but Rudy was in hell based on his strained grunts and eye rolls.

"Good job, pretty baby," he moaned. "You look so beautiful with my dick down yo throat, Cheré."

Men lied a lot when they were in love. Cause my eyes were watering while I gagged and there was spit dripping down my chest and pooling at my knees. Pretty? Doubtful. Primal? Probably.

His hand-gathered all the curls hanging from the back and middle of my head while my hands gripped his shaft to spread my spit. I knew he was likely hanging on by a thread but I didn't care to stop. I was too busy enjoying the way my release tasted on his clean skin. I was too busy inhaling his scent while he twitched in my mouth. I was too busy getting lost in him. Eventually, he got lost in me too. He was moaning, cussing, and whimpering. Then he bit that thick bottom lip and that's when I knew I was about to make Rudy Jones cum.

"Cher, slow down," he mumbled.

It was opposite day in my mind so I sped up instead, bracing myself for whatever consequences would follow.

"Duchess, I said slow down," he hissed.

I continued to ignore him and his hand tightened around the arm of the rocker while I continued. He was so hard it would hurt if I didn't get off on having my throat fucked. But I did, especially when it was him. I swallowed as much of his throbbing dick as my mouth would allow while relishing the sensation of my swollen lips stretching around him, then I heard the wood creak before it splintered in Rudy's hand. He broke a $400 rocking chair like it was a Popsicle stick. Sure, I could've scolded him, but that would've been real hard considering my cheeks were full of gooey hot cum. Rudy bucked uncontrollably, flooding my mouth with his release while I swallowed every last drop like the good girl I was. Yeah, that shit was fun, real fun.

Sometimes I get ahead of myself. Usually, I notice pretty immediately, but not this time. I remember smiling at Rudy and ejecting my tongue to show off my empty mouth, but now my face was being pressed against the white shag carpet in front of the couch while Rudy buried his tongue in my ass. It felt good, too good. The type of good that made me wanna say fuck my degree and move back to Texas. So I tried to move against my better judgment, and the action was swiftly met with a flat-out refusal. Rudy reunited me with the floor and held me there with his left hand while his right occupied my pussy. So now there was a hot tongue probing my tight asshole, big fingers inside me, and a thumb circling my clit while my nipples rubbed against the carpet.

I was getting overwhelmed again. All because I didn't listen when he told me to slow down. I thought I was ready to handle the consequences, but I was still naive when it came to Rudy Jones. And I knew it as soon as my vision split from one of the strongest orgasms of my life. I was seeing triple and the light from the fire morphed into something bright and blinding while my eyes squeezed shut. Like I said, I got ahead of myself.

Rudy waited until my legs stopped vibrating to lift me from the ground, and I was still ready to go despite my seven minutes in hell. Anyone normal would be satisfied but my pussy ached to be filled by our favorite person. So I tried to push Rude on the already violated couch. However, he didn't budge. The mountain of a man stood there staring at me while I exhausted my efforts to top him, and then he grabbed my waist and pulled me flush to him.

"No, Cher," he murmured while sucking my earlobe.

I didn't understand him at times. He told me no, yet he was still getting me hot and bothered. My mind melted under the heat of his cinnamon breath. I was in another place. A place filled with vivid, rainbow-colored dick kaleidoscopes and Rudy Jones's lips. Lips I wanted pressed against mine right then. I was frustrated, and I was gone have a meltdown if I didn't get him inside me soon.

"Why not?" I cried, unable to hide the desperation in my tone.

"Because," Rudy said, smiling a knowing smile.

"Because what?" I pouted.

Rudy swept a few curls out my face and tucked them behind my ears before laying me against a blanket he spread on the brick hearth. His warm body pressed against mine, silently demanding submission while he fulfilled my need to kiss, and I drowned in his tender pecks before he pulled away to reply,

"Because you were on top last time," he answered, easing into me.

Father God in Heaven above, I hoped this wasn't the time my people decided to watch over me. Cause the sight of us would've given my Nana a second heart attack. I hoped there was CPR in heaven. My knees were touching my shoulders and Rudy Jones was taking full advantage of my compromised position. I was wide open and stretched out like taffy. Then his warm tongue swirled against the pad of my first three toes while he fucked me into the ground. His thumb never lost its motion on my clit, and when he was done sucking me like Sonic ice, his gaze consumed mine.

It was official. I didn't know up from down or left from right. I suddenly couldn't remember the date, and if you woulda asked me what state we were in, I probably woulda answered Mars. All I knew for sure was that Rudy Jones felt good inside me and that his lip quivered when I scratched the left side of his scalp.

He changed directions and a moan ripped through the late-night air, making me blush from how well it echoed off the high ceilings. It sounded so desperate. It sounded like a wounded deer or a feral mating call. Then it was so loud and throaty that I couldn't even recognize myself.

"Rudy Jones, what are you doing to me?" I panted.

Rudy slowed his stroke to bury his nose in the crook of my neck instead of immediately answering. But he revisited the topic after a couple of tender kisses and a few deeply obnoxious sniffs.

"Lovin' you," he replied.

My nipples pebbled the second the words left his mouth. He was loving me. He was also sucking the shit outta my diamond-hard nipples, but he was still loving me. Caressing me, holding me, kissing me, and stroking me. Rudy lifted my back and our tempo slowed enough for me to watch him pump in and out of me. I was curious cause it sounded like somebody was whipping butter into a pot of grits. The motion in his hips was fluid and sensuous while he stroked on a one-half beat reminiscent of I Wanna Know, I could see how much my pink contrasted with his dark brown while I creamed him, and my pussy gripped around him so tight that I had to stop watching to prevent from passing out.

Then Rudy pulled my leg higher around his waist to get closer. I think I was closer to nirvana than I was to real life because my entire person craved being one with him. It always had.

"Rudy Jones, I ain't never stopped loving you either," I confessed.

Rudy's eyes got wide before an unusually nervous grin appeared on his lips. Then he leaned in close to my lips while cupping my reddened cheek.

"I'm way too simple for you to be saying things like that while I'm swimming in you, Duchess," he chuckled.

Our foreheads were pressed together while I clung to his back, and our bodies moved harmoniously against the warmed stone beneath us. I watched the fire dance in his earthen eyes while we twined, and I was one step closer to my goal of being completely lost in Rudy Jones.

"I mean it," I panted, tears streaming down my face.

Rudy used his thumb to dry my eyes while kissing the top of my head. Then he looked back at me with tears forming in his own eyes.

I wiped them before they even had the chance to trail his cheeks and Rudy nuzzled my hand appreciatively.

"I know, Noah. I know baby," he cried.

I heard the thirty-second countdown when I started to peak. 2023 was almost over, and I had ended the year in one of the most unexpected ways; wrapped around my husband after wasting far too many years apart.

I pushed my hips flush to Rudy's while the TV crowd counted down from ten.

"Ten!"

"Duchess," Rudy panted, biting through that bottom lip.

"Nine!"

"I'm a big girl, Rude. I can take it," I assured.

"Eight!"

Rudy grabbed my chin desperately, raising my gaze to meet his.

"Duchess."

I locked eyes with him at his command, effectively sealing my fate. I drowned in a glass of cognac so fine that Hennessy couldn't hold a candle to it. My mind disintegrated, allowing my body to take the reins. Then my body dissolved, melting into something unrecognizable as bliss ripped me apart and stitched me back together. I watched the entire process in Rudy Jones's eyes while he did the same thing. We were falling apart together. Drowning in more ways than one.

Then, as the heirloom grandfather clock struck midnight, we got lost in each other. Unraveling six years of self-inflicted torture. I let my chaotic, pitchy, moan fill the first morning of the new year while Rude filled me. I missed the feeling so much that I came again while he twitched against my tender inside. Damn, Rudy Jones. We caught our breath while he brushed the wild, tangled, mass of curls out of my eyes. Then he slowly leaned forward to place a gentle peck on my swollen lips.

"Happy New Year, Duchess," he smiled anxiously.

I smiled back at him just as nervously before reaching to stroke his warm nape.

"Happy New Year, Rudy Jones," I whispered.

Rudy

This morning was a dream. Honestly, the whole week was, but this morning I woke up in the big bed with Noah drawing soft circles on my chest. With the sun rising lazily behind us, I let her map a path to her favorite places before I took one last visit to mine. I guess she still hadn't decided if I was worth the inevitable headache, but I was ok with that. Because at least she let me hold her tight before we started the day. She was so warm and so soft. Plus she smelled like a well-maintained library that had lavender hanging from the walls. It was a peace unlike any other. So I was ok with that one last gift. I had to be.

"Gotcha chargers?" I asked.

Noah checked her big tote and pulled out the bundle of cords for verification.

"Yep!"

"Even your vibrator ones?" I double-checked.

She narrowed her eyes at me menacingly before looking back into the wire bundles.

"Yes, Rude," she snickered.

"Good. Wouldn't want Agnes growling at folks in a week," I said, patting just above her pussy.

"Boy, bye!" she tutted, pushing off my chest. "You do too much, Rudy Jones!"

God, I loved it when she said my name like that. Even though she was fed the fuck up with me. Even though we were leaving.

"Ok, let me grab your bags so we can get going," I mumbled.

Noah's big eyes somehow got bigger, and she stepped closer to examine my expression.

"Where are we going?" she asked.

I'm greedy, so I took the opportunity to hold her little hand and tuck some of her soft curls behind her ear before answering.

"To the airport, Cher. You live in New York, remember?"

Noah slowly backed down with a quivering bottom lip. Was that disappointment on her face? Nah, couldn't be. Maybe I was just being annoying. I heard I was good at that.

"Oh, I… I just thought I was catching a Lyft," she mumbled.

Noah had $282 in her bank account. I know because I grimaced when I accidentally seent it this morning. A Lyft an hour away would at least be half of that. So yeah, I was driving her, and I was definitely paying that high-ass rent.

"Nah, Duchess. I ain't finna have you Lyfting shit but ya skirt if you want to. Come on, baby. Let's get you back to yo life," I said, more defeat lingering in my tone than I wanted.

Noah nodded and maybe reluctantly turned around. I think my mind was just playing tricks on me though. Cause who would be mad about a free ride?

Then she spun around on her heels, snapping my attention up.

"It's just!" she started. "Fuck!"

Ok, maybe I was wrong. Maybe she was mad about the ride. She had me wondering if I was being dismissive and patronizing.

She practically charged at me. Her long legs pushed full speed ahead until her ample chest bumped into mine. And damn, if I wasn't drained from that morning, I probably would've came in my pants. But I refocused because Duchess was scowling at me, and I wanted to know what was wrong.

"No, baby. What I do?" I asked.

Noah chewed her bottom lip furiously. Chomping it like Mike did when he bit Holyfield's ear off. Then she looked up at me, eyes just as curious and demanding.

"Tell me your New Year's resolution," she said plainly.

"What?" I mumbled.

Noah hooked her pointer finger under my chin, tilting my head to meet her gaze before she asked me again.

"Tell me your New Year's resolution, Rudy Jones," she demanded.

Now I was biting my lip because I ain't never had a resolution in my thirty-one years of living, but I did this year and I hadn't planned on sharing.

Noah kissed her teeth, clearly irritated by my silence. Her nose scrunched, her eyes darted around, then she pinched the bridge of her nose before cussing under her breath. I thought she would head back to the truck but her pretty glossy lips parted instead.

"I like you, Rudolph Jones. I like you real bad," she announced. "And I get the feeling that you might like me. So since we like each other, we should go together."

I think my heart stopped beating for a second because my brain sure as hell blacked out. Noah liked me. She wanted to go with me. I had a fucking chance with my wife. I ain't know what to say so I did the only thing that felt right. I completely disregarded my busted ass rib and lifted Noah off the ground to kiss her. Then I thanked God above for answering all my midnight prayers. I was getting my wife back, I was getting my partner back, and most importantly, I was getting my friend back. I was about to pass out before I remembered I needed air to breathe. So since I needed to stop kissing to get air, I pulled away to catch Noah's smile gleaming in the daylight.

"Getting you back was my New Year's resolution," I confessed. "Losing you was the biggest mistake of my life."

Noah nodded while hot tears ran down her face and cut through her mascara. Her wild curls tickled my neck and face while she left lil nervous kisses on my forehead, and then she laughed. Her laugh was so bright. It was brighter than the perfect white snow that was falling all around us. It was brighter than whatever ring I could ever possibly buy her. And it was bright like our future. The one with communication, support, mutual understanding, and lots of sex that would probably lead to some equally bright babies.

"Then I think 2024 has been successful for both of us, Rudy Jones," she whispered.

I wasn't one to count my chickens before they hatched, but for Noah? I counted the whole fucking farm before ever laying eyes on it.

"You right, Noah. I know you are, baby," I whispered.

Noah kissed the end of my nose and I melted into her fully and without reservations. Yeah, 2024 was gonna be a year for the records, and I was glad. Real glad.

Nine

Epilogue

Rudy

You know what I never found romantic? The way I proposed to Noah the first time. Clearly, she ain't feel that way because she said yes, but it still bothered me. Even then. Especially now. It was in the damn gym at senior prom. The room was dim and sketchy, and it still smelled like a sweat sock despite the gallon of purple Fabuloso lingering on the scratched floors. Then a hundred people were staring at us. Waiting. I had social anxiety. Noah had social anxiety. My dumb ass had a ring that looked like a Superbowl memento. It was a shit show, but I also knew she truly loved me, because she really should have laughed in my young dumb face.

But that's ok, cause it's never too late to right a wrong. It had been a year since my lil plot, and things were going well. We did long-distance for the first three months, but I couldn't take it after having to fly home and leave her there immediately after Valentine's day. So I packed up my shit, put the house up for rent, and high-tailed it back to Noah. After her graduation in May, we found an apartment that didn't look like an abused changing room in Harlem, moved in together, and even got a cat. She was jet black with one white paw and a crooked ear. So naturally we named her Crookshank. We were killing it in couple's therapy, Noah was having a blast decorating and buying plants she eventually murdered, I was eating a concerning amount of onion gravy, and Nala was saying I told you so at every opportunity. So fuck well, things were going great, and I was glad. Real glad.

We were back in New York after spending Christmas week at Heaven's Peak, and holy fuck, I completely understood why she just ain't fly home early last year. I think I heard my wallet physically holler when I booked the tickets. Then again, my baby was worth it. Plus I wanted her to be more comfortable than the first time, and the free fireworks show visible from our balcony didn't hurt either. I poured her and myself a generous glass of Moscato before turning on Maxwell, and we rocked while the city behind us descended into complete debauchery and chaos. Eleven thirty struck, and I put the countdown on the living room TV so we could keep track of time. That step was crucial because Noah was fixin' to be turned inside out before I noticed it was only five minutes until. My plan was time-sensitive, so I ushered into our room to do my mad dash. "Be right back," I called.

I had hidden about eighty candles around the house with Nala's assistance, so I lit those first before arranging my pile of rose petals into a heart at the balcony door. I finished with just two minutes to spare and I opened the door to find Noah's nosey ass stumbling back, likely trying to see if she could hear what was happening.

"Come on, Cher," I chuckled. "Let's watch the fireworks."

She laughed and followed me until she couldn't. Her motion stopped abruptly since her feet were likely stuck in place from the sight of things. She did that a lot when she was excited.

"Rudy," she gasped. "What is this?"

Her eyes followed the perimeter of the room, taking everything in before her gaze rejoined mine. She was nervous, maybe even cautious, and that wouldn't do.

"Just wanted to thank you for last year, Duchess," I shrugged.

I picked her up bridal style and carried her over to the heart. The roses were the perfect shade of burgundy, and they matched my baby's pretty dress. Apparently, she had her eye on it for a while back in Heaven's Peak, and luckily it was just her size. She only had to get some minor alterations to keep her bust from spilling out, but she could've truthfully gone without that, in my humbly perverted opinion.

My pulse shot up while I stared into those big, curious, maple-brown eyes. Her interest coated me like I was a plate of hot pancakes and shit, maybe I was from the way her eyes darted to my crotch and back up. I think I ruined her last year, cause she had been unhinged since we both climaxed at the stroke of midnight. It was a magic she wanted to replicate at any given chance, and I wasn't gone stop her, except for right now.

"Focus on the task at hand, baby," I reminded her.

Noah nodded, still staring at my dick before I lifted her chin manually. Then she flashed me that megawatt smile.

"Right. Which is?"

"The countdown," I answered.

She sucked in a sharp breath, seemingly remembering what day it was.

"Right, I'm focusing," she nodded.

We counted in sync while she twirled her hips to the music playing softly in the background.

"Five, four, three, two…"

I dropped to my knees at one, revealing a kite-shaped emerald ring that I had been keeping in my shirt pockets for weeks. I had asked her what her favorite gemstone was in January under the ploy of a Valentine's day gift, and to my surprise, she answered emerald. When I asked her why, she just said,

"They're so pretty, and the color always reminds me of you."

If I wasn't in love before, I definitely was then. There were only a few thousand miles stopping me from packing her ass up and doing this shit Vegas style, but I was already righting a wrong, and this time I wasn't gonna fuck up the plan.

Noah noticed the rock and gasped before clutching her racing heart. Her chest was heaving and the tears were pouring out of her eyes before I could even get the words out.

"Noah Tyler Harrison-Jones," I started. "You got this thing you do when you nervous. Sometimes you talk to yourself about it, but most of the time your eyes dart around like you looking at a maze or a puzzle. That's how I be knowing when you overthinking."

She asked me how I knew months ago, but I shrugged it off, not wanting to reveal my secret just then.

"So, yeah. I know you nervous, and I know you probably overthinking, but I just want you to answer however feels right. No matter how you think I'll f…"

Noah cut me off with a simple wave before placing her hand against my cheek.

"Rudy Jones, stop talking," she mumbled. "Ask me what you wanna ask me."

I swallowed with my nerves more jumbled than ever before. Even more than that time I took my audacious ass to Colorado after the holidays and ambushed my wife. But I pushed that shit down and focused, eager to meet her bratty-ass demand.

"Noah, Cheré. Will you please marry my nerve-wracking ass?" I pleaded. "I promise I won't fuck up this time."

Noah's expression didn't change until I realized her strong legs were straddling my waist. She had knocked my big ass down onto the floor so quick it made my head spin. I held my breath because I was struggling to keep my hold on the ring and my composure while she kissed my neck and chin affectionately. If she ain't give me an answer soon, my dick was gone provide one for her.

"Yes, Rudy Jones. I'll marry you," she laughed. "Again."

"Oh, thank God," I sighed. "A nigga was about to pass out."

I slipped the ring on her delicate lil finger, admiring how much better it looked than the first one. It suited her better. It suited us better. Me and my wife who was about to officially and legally be my wife again.

Noah yawned, coaxing an equally exhausted yawn from my mouth. We had been celebrating my birthday non-stop the entire week, and them brunch mimosas were coming back to haunt me. As excited as I was, I was honestly fine if Noah was overwhelmed and decided she needed rest. However, her lil ass was full of surprises. She leaned down to whisper against my lips, letting those wild curls fall in my face while I watched a small fire light in her eyes.

"Wanna make a baby?" she asked.

I noticed that fire was spreading, and it was getting harder to ask clarifying questions by the second. It was getting harder in general.

"Like for real, or pretendsy?" I inquired anxiously.

I ain't wanna get too excited. We both had a thing for the occasional creampie, but we limited that treat to right before her periods to avoid pregnancy.

Noah smiled before taking my earlobe into her mouth. Then she ran her tongue over my piercing while I writhed underneath her, accidentally brushing my hard against her soft and noticeably wet thong.

"For real," she chuckled innocently. "I had my IUD removed two months ago."

Welp, I guess I had my New Year's resolution for 2025. A nigga was about to be a daddy in more ways than one, and I was excited. Real excited.

Thank You!

Thank you so much for taking the time to read Rudy and Noah's story. This is my third book and my first novella. I worked hard to preserve my writing style although it's shorter than the other two. You may notice that the overall structure of how I write is changing, and that's because I'm listening to your valued feedback. So please consider rating and reviewing this book if you have the time. It helps other readers find my work, and it helps me improve. Thanks again, and I hope to see you in the next one!

Glory Sneak Peak

My name is Gloria, and I think I'm a succubus. I know they're not *technically* real, but if they were, I'd be their leader. I love everything associated with orgasms, especially men's. I like feeling their hot cum sticking to my used holes. I like hearing their ragged breath whimper my praises, and I especially like when they get overwhelmed and bow their backs, eager to release their frustrations. It soothes my depraved hungry mind for a few days so I can continue to dominate at work and support my community. It gives me back the power taken from me by these ridiculous societal expectations, and it's damn fun. So that's why I think I'm a succubus. Because I, Gloria Esther King, pull my strength from the sins of men, instead of the glory of God.

But before you assume it's because someone touched me, or I use drugs, or because my parents let me run wild, never setting a boundary or saying no, let me clarify some things. The House Of King is a good Christian house where I had a stern, but loving, upbringing. My father comes from a long line of pastors and my mother from an equally long line of schoolteachers. Their union yielded four children, with my siblings being standard-issue and mostly mild-mannered. So the problem is definitely me.

My mother first noticed it when I was about seven. I would doodle little obscenities in the margins of my notebooks, mostly breast. Ink-drawn tits were basically my signature for quite a while, but my mother wasn't worried. She must have shrugged it off as simple self-curiosity until it evolved into something worse in my pre-teens. Big, veiny, hairy dicks. She had the same concerns as most. She was worried that someone had exposed me to something or themselves, and that's where my perversions stemmed from, but the truth was much worse. She and my father spent nearly two weeks trying to coax a statement out of me that simply didn't exist. And while I was happy to leave it, I knew I had to be honest when they started questioning my brother.

Marcus still stands as one of the two only people I've ever loved outside my parents. He was a good big brother when we were kids. Picking on me when necessary, strengthening me for the real world, and protecting me always. I'm still his pride and joy to this day, and that's why I'd never let his character be called into judgment. I remember my stomach tightening with anxiety and fear before my cracked lips parted to tell the truth.

"No one touched me! I was watching the men's locker room!" I shouted.

There was a hole barely big enough for a rat to squeeze through in our church's upstairs study room. It was so small that the only evidence of its existence was the light that peered through when you moved the chair over in the dark. I noticed it one day after kissing a little boy from my youth group. He hurried away when the pastor called, and I stayed behind to practice more doodles. I doodled often on Sundays. My father was strict, but even he could understand a young mind's tendency to wander. So he left me upstairs after the third sermon to draw. I followed the same routine as usual that day. Kiss a boy, wait for him to panic, then draw, but when I moved the chair to get comfortable, I found something else worthy of my time. *Dicks.* There was a shower room downstairs for our homeless members and clergymen. It braved heavy traffic on Sundays, especially in the summer, so I spent three months of my time memorizing the privates of its frequent flyers. Especially brother Myer-Smythe. His dick was my favorite. Veiny, thick, long, and drooping over his balls like a partially deflated balloon animal. My mother nearly fainted while I fought to keep the smile off my face, and my father curled his fist into a tight ball. Yeah, I'm the problem.

My daddy had the hole repaired, and my access to privacy was of course revoked. But that didn't stop my fascination with penises. I often tried to bribe Marcus' friends to show me theirs with the little bit of allowance I got, and while I was lucky half the time, Franklin Myer-Smythe eventually snubbed my luck by snitching on me. At just four years my senior, he felt he was suited to tell me how I ought to behave. And while his concerns did have some merit, he was mostly full of shit. He was mad about his boyfriend. So after he blew up my spot, I was confined to solitude while my parents searched for a solution through God. But after many, many, failed attempts at correcting my behavior through prayer, they turned to science.

Turns out Zoloft worked faster than the Lord above us could, and I spent my teen years dedicated to a strict routine to curb my urges. It's been fourteen years since I started meds, and while I was upset at first, I can admit they helped me. I graduated as a high school salutatorian, a college valedictorian, and a law school prodigy, highly desired by both of my chosen specialties. I was offered the best jobs, got the greatest benefits, plus I have a pretty good life. And I owe it all to a little orange pill that dries my pussy up like a dream deferred.

But I'm grown now, and at the ripe age of 27, I decided that I wasn't going to be ashamed of my hyper sexuality. Especially after hearing dozens of stories of other women having issues with the opposite. I decided to embrace my insatiable lust and go with it. I am who I am, and I am a whore. So I skip my meds Thursday and Friday nights, put on my tightest dress and highest heels, and head into town to have some damn good fun. I've had a thing for glory holes lately, and it might just be the name, but I can't help myself. Using some faceless schlub as a dildo is the perfect way to end a hectic week, especially if I lose a case. I usually find a seedy club or swingers bar to scratch my itch, but I've taken on a different challenge recently. *Gay bars.* Gay bars have the best glory holes. Triple-lined with duct tape, clean, and condoms are usually provided. Plus I like that gay men keep their dicks clean. Clean dicks taste better, especially when they cum down my throat. It was finally Friday, and tonight was no exception. I put on a skintight leather dress, a pair of heels that could make a seasoned dominatrix keel, and lined my lips with sinfully red lipstick. Yeah, tonight was gonna be good.

I arrived at Adam And Steve's a quarter after nine and it was already packed. Luckily, I knew Adam personally, so I got to skip right past the thick security guard who wouldn't give me his number and head inside. I didn't jump straight into it though. I nursed a margarita while watching the crowd. A sea of moisturized and glittering bodies were busy rippling against each other, entrancing me. Especially the fems. If I wasn't violently craving dick I probably would have gone after the cute brown skin fem with the neon purple hair. She looked fun and soft, but I needed something hard for tonight.

I finished my drinks around 10:30 and decided to make my way to the men's room. Hopefully, no one paid me too much mind, and if they did, hopefully they assumed I was trans. That thought made my mind wander to the last trans girlie I met. Her dick was tattooed and she had a fat ass. *"Focus Gloria!"* I told myself. This wasn't about Sonni, it was about tonight. Me, a sketchy hole, and an equally sketchy penis. Bad decisions all around. Not cute girls who wanted a cat, a girlfriend, and matching Christmas pajamas. No, no, no.

I try not to get into relationships if I can help it. Sometimes situationships get close, but I usually nip it in the bud before anyone can get hurt. Contrary to popular belief, I do have a heart, and the last thing I want is to open up to someone and have them spit on it because I'm sexually non-monogamous. So I just decided to bypass all of that and cuddle my best friend on occasion, let my family absorb my free time, and suck dicks and eat coochies until my jaw hurts. That way every human need is taken care of, and I never let things get out of hand with my lil friends.

Anyway, back to tonight. I got comfortable in the big stall while I waited. A few people ran in and out, but I still didn't have a contender after an hour. I was almost ready to pack it up and try the direct approach, but then I heard my calling card. A zipper and no urine stream proceeding it. Finally, it was showtime. Most frequent fliers knew about the glory hole, including Adam. So naturally, there was a laminated instruction card taped inside both stalls. I knocked on the divider once and the person knocked back twice, indicating that they wanted to play. So I kicked a condom under the thin space between our stalls and eagerly waited for a response.

My Dick Donor must've also been eager because they ripped that pack and knocked back in record time. I knocked twice, indicating I was ready, but I don't think I could ever be ready for what I saw. A big head pushed through the hole before the rest fell over to my side, and it was perfect. It was deep brown, heavy in my hand, with veins on the surface straining against the condom, plus it was uncut. It was rare to see an uncut dick nowadays, but they were my absolute favorite. It jumped at me, demanding my attention, and I narrowed my eyes at it. I knew I never had it, but it looked oddly familiar. It also looked like a challenge. I normally stuck to a head-only rule for lil holes in the walls, but I think I would pass away if I didn't at least try to back down this one.

So I braced myself on the wall in front of me and eased down Goliath's dick. I was soaking wet, but I didn't have any other choice but to go slow. Cause when the head entered me, I had to throw my hand over my mouth to contain my yelp. Shit, big was somehow an understatement. I'm not real religious anymore, but I had to call on The Father, The Spirit, and The Holy Ghost to make it down their length. I was perfectly full and stretched to the max, which was honestly rare for me. I liked dicks of all sizes, but I was accustomed to medium ones. Not backbreakers.

I finally reached the base and Captain Dingle groaned and cussed, saying something about how tight I was. I loved dirty talk, but my voice was way too recognizable. It was high-pitched and shrill, just like my schoolteacher mama. So unless I wanted to deny my truth and have folks thinking my mama was running around utilizing local glory holes, I kept my mouth shut. That didn't stop me from humming with relief though. My shit was throbbing every time I thrusted against that big ass dick. Plus it didn't hurt that my donor was meeting my pace by stroking back. I could imagine them being an absolute menace without a barrier between us, so it was a good thing that wasn't an option.

The first rule of hypersexuality was to never expect too much from your partners. Most people were normal, and they got their serotonin from shit like hobbies and hugs, so they never wanted it as much as you. They never needed it. Never craved it. But my donor had blown my expectations outta the sky. It had been ten minutes and we were still going. I know because I heard three different songs come over the speakers and at least six different folks shuffle in and out, some cheering on our debauchery. I think they wanted it too, and fuck, that shit was hot.

Six songs had played since we started and we were still at it, but I needed it to stop because I was about to pass out. They were making me cum. I think they might've even been doing it on purpose because they used whatever sliver of room they had to change angles repeatedly. It was rare that I came during penetration without toys, and it was even rarer that a stranger had my wetness rushing down my shaky legs. They switched angles again, making the hinges on the stall groan as they did, and I was fighting a losing battle against containing my moans. So I let out a little pant with my next cresting wave of pleasure before it crashed down and ruined me.

That was a mistake though, because my donor showed their ass as soon as I did. They rammed into me so hard that I almost lost my balance, and I had to grip the toilet paper holder to remain upright. Then I made another mistake by trying to catch their rhythm because it was far too superior to anything I was used to. So there my dumb dickmatized ass was, struggling not to moan while a horse-dicked stranger knocked the Mario coins out my shit. Then as if things wasn't bad enough, their shit got harder, the strokes got faster, and my pussy clenched tighter. *Oh no.* I thought. The pressure overwhelmed me before I realized what was happening. My stomach tightened while warm liquid sprayed out of me, soaking the floor, my donor, and myself. I had fucking squirted in a public bathroom. The insatiable whore in me didn't know rather to be impressed or ashamed, but who could tell since she had been temporarily relieved of duty.

My donor's orgasm succeeded mine, making me cum one last time before they withdrew their sticky twitching dick, and a bitch was spent. I was a sweaty, shaking, crumpled mess. My body hurt and I was out of breath, and I was also completely sexually satisfied. Usually, I was the one doing the fucking, but someone had fucked me. It was a perfect night of rare encounters, and I owed it all to Adam's nasty ass, a roll of duct tape, and a perfect stranger.

I caught my breath and fixed myself in the little door mirror while I waited for my donor to leave. Good dick aside, I needed them to stay a stranger. The kind of sex we had was dangerous and had the tendency to complicate things, and I was in no mood for complicated. I eventually heard the lock on their door click open and light from their exit flooded the pleasure chute that was still dripping with my cum. Yeah, I needed to tell Adam about that. Bleach was needed.

One song later, the water stopped running, the door swung open, and my donor left with a loud, but satisfied sigh. For some reason that made me blush, and I had to shake off the weirdly warm feeling before opening my door. No, thank you to whatever that was. That exchange was supposed to be purely physical, and that warmth felt real emotional. I decided I was gonna numb that with a shot or two before heading home. I was taking a self-care day the next day anyway, so it'd be easy to nurse my hangover. But that plan was ruined as soon as I exited my stall and looked up.

Shit had gotten complicated.

About the Author

Aria is a die-hard romantic and her main goal is to always be drying her eyes from something sickly sweet. She has been dreaming up romance stories since she was seven years old, with the first one being a Toy Story fanfic. Her dream is to one day write inclusive stories that center BIPOC full-time, but for now, she labors in fraud as a working stay-at-home mom.

She's also a Neo-soul and R&B enthusiast who's forever got a song stuck in her head. You can find her looking for good food, reading, writing, or enjoying time with her family in her free time. She lives happily in Saint Louis, Missouri with her middle school sweetheart-turned-husband and their adorably chaotic son.

You can connect with me on:

- https://dazedreamers.com
- https://www.instagram.com/ariadazewrites
- https://www.tiktok.com/@authorariadaze

Bloom

Winifred Walsh is sick of perfect. She's sick of speeches, estate dinners, coordinated undergarments, and dealing with the "perfect" man. Unfortunately, she could never picture anything else for her life, so she was committed to the end. That is until she met Marvin. He's intelligent, handsome, kind, and everything she was raised to avoid. A working-class white man the blue eyes and no money. Her father has made it clear that she is a representative of their family first and foremost, which meant no partying, no boyfriends, and certainly no sex. But the Heiress quickly realizes that making the most out of life means leaving some parts of herself behind, including her not-so-humble beginnings. Set in the early 70s, Bloom details the challenges a young Marvin Rosenbloom and his wife, Winifred face before Rosencorp and strict employee dating policies. Join them on a story filled with scandal, murder, and sex as they start their lives together.

Candid

Wilhelmina Sturges is not looking for Mr. Right. She has no desire to give up her independence or share her space with someone else. But that starts to change when she meets Thebes.

Thebes Dacres hates socializing, he hates conversation, and he especially hates touching. His disdain for affection knows no bounds, and that's why he's still a virgin at 31 years old. No one ever expected him to get married or fall in love, himself included. But he quickly realizes that life isn't as predictable as he'd like to believe.

Wilhelmina's smart, she's stunning, and she makes his heart beat fast. Attraction is something Thebes never experienced, and their instant chemistry often gets them into trouble. Especially when they realize he's her new boss. But Thebes can't help but risk it all for Wilhelmina, and she must decide if she'll reciprocate.